A DEAL WITH ALEJANDRO

BY

MAYA BLAKE

MILLS & BOON

First published in Great Britain 2016
By Mills & Boon, an imprint of HarperCollins*Publishers*
1 London Bridge Street, London, SE1 9GF

Large Print edition 2017

© 2016 Maya Blake

ISBN: 978-0-263-07060-6

Printed and bound in Great Britain
by CPI Antony Rowe, Chippenham, Wiltshire

CHAPTER ONE

ALEJANDRO AGUILAR STEPPED out of a bracing, ice-cold shower to the sound of a ringing phone. At 4:00 a.m. such an occurrence would have alarmed most people. He already had a fair idea of why his early-morning routine was being disturbed.

Crossing the master bedroom suite of his Chicago penthouse, he draped the towel round his neck and picked up the phone.

'Is it done?'

A muted sigh from his chief strategist, Wendell Grant, greeted him. 'I'm sorry, sir, but they wouldn't be swayed. We've thrown everything at them, including my firstborn son.'

The attempt at humour fell flat, causing the weary-sounding man to clear his throat uncomfortably.

Alejandro's grip tightened on the handset, the inkling he'd harboured for several weeks expanding to nape-tingling certainty. There were far too many indicators to ignore the suspicion any longer.

'Frankly, I'm at a loss as to why they've suddenly

become so intransigent,' Wendell continued. 'The Ishikawa brothers' team refuses to even discuss what the problem is beyond stating that they need more time.'

Alejandro knew what the problem was. The heads of the Japanese e-commerce conglomerate were protracting the deal, which should've been final-ised a month ago, in order to accommodate a third party's interest.

'How did you leave things?' he asked.

'They've asked for a few more days. We tried to get an earlier date but they wouldn't budge. We've agreed to a videoconference on Friday.'

'That's unacceptable. I'm not waiting another five days. Call them back. Tell them I want the Ishikawa brothers in conference tomorrow.'

'Yes, sir.'

About to hang up, Alejandro sensed his execu-tive's reticence. 'Is there something else?'

'Well...I got the feeling they think they have the upper hand. The dynamic has definitely shifted...'

Hearing his suspicions voiced by another brought a clench of anger to Alejandro's gut. If his execu-tives had sniffed out the same issue, it was time to take over the helm again.

'Sir? Is there something we should know?'

Alejandro squashed his ire. 'I'll take it from here.

Extend my gratitude to the team and tell everyone to take the day off. You've earned it.'

'You still want me to make the call?' Wendell asked.

'No. I'll take care of it.' Now that he knew with whom he was dealing, it was time the gloves came off.

'If you're sure, then I better get home to my wife before she serves me with divorce papers.' Another weary laugh, which fizzled away, the other man sensing Alejandro's tense mood. 'Oh, one last thing. I had my assistant compile the shortlist of PR firms for you. Jameson PR has the most extensive experience in Asia. I think at this stage we need all the help we can get.'

Alejandro finished the call and hung up. Snatching the towel from around his neck, he dropped it and padded naked to his dressing room. His signature grey suits, black shirts and bespoke pinstripe ties were within easy reach. Selecting a charcoal suit, he dressed with military efficiency, and was heading out of the door fifteen minutes later.

The drive to the Loop, the financial heart of Chicago, took less than ten minutes. The early hour meant very little traffic and Alejandro gained marginal satisfaction from letting the engine of his Bugatti Veyron roar along the quiet streets.

But nothing could ease the iron-hard fist of unwelcome knowledge trapped in his gut. Nor the accompanying rage that mounted with each passing second.

He'd moved from Spain, the country of his birth, to California at the age of twenty-one, and then relocated to Chicago a year after that because he'd wanted nothing to do with his family. The move from Spain had been to remove himself as soon as it was legally possible from the volatile quagmire that was his parents' sham of a marriage. Alejandro had put several thousand miles between himself and the two individuals biology had used to create him, and never looked back. Little did he know he'd been placing himself within touching distance of another powder keg in the form of his half-brother.

Gael Aguilar.

He was half of the equation that had worsened the acrimony in Alejandro's life over two decades ago. Gael and his mother had put faces on the hitherto faceless monsters that were his father's indiscretions. Those monsters had grown until Alejandro had had no choice but to leave the only home he'd known.

But the nightmare hadn't been ready to let him be.

Gael had arrived in California shortly after him.

And Silicon Valley hadn't been large enough to contain the two of them. Especially when his younger half-brother had started making himself a nuisance by going after the same deals Alejandro showed interest in. Wiping out Gael's burgeoning e-commerce start-up would've been an easy accomplishment for Alejandro. But that would've indicated he cared one iota about the life he'd put behind him. It would've given the impression that the countless instances of infidelity, rancour and falsehood that had peppered his childhood still had the power to matter.

So he'd walked away.

He might be an Aguilar, but he was so in name only. Nothing about it was worthy of being lauded. He'd cut all ties. As far as he was concerned, he existed in this world alone.

Except his half-brother hadn't got the memo. A decade after meeting for the second and final time, it appeared Gael was determined to insert himself into Alejandro's business once again. Or at the very least, scurry away with the deal Alejandro had worked tirelessly to pull together.

Turning off his engine, he launched himself from the car and crossed the underground car park of his company's building. Entering the lift that would take him to the top-floor offices of SNV International, he recalled that last exchange with his brother when Gael had found out he was leaving California.

'I hear you're relocating your business. Why? You scared I'm going to show you up?' Gael's white smile, cocksure, taunting and tinged with bravado, had reminded Alejandro too much of their father's, eliciting nothing but cold indifference.

'Don't kid yourself. My company is successful enough to thrive anywhere in the world. But perhaps you should count your lucky stars that I'm leaving and removing myself from the temptation to crush you into the dirt. This way you at least have a hope of making something of yourself.'

His brother's smile had evaporated like mist in sunshine. A look Alejandro had ironically recognised in himself—one of implacable will and determination—had passed over Gael's features.

'I look forward to the day when I make you swallow those words, *hermano*.'

Alejandro had shrugged and walked away. He hadn't bothered to tell Gael they would never be true brothers because they'd never meet again. Crossing paths once when they were teenagers had been bad enough. A second time, in their twenties, was overkill.

He'd thought there wouldn't be a third.

Except, walking away hadn't ended it. Foolishly, it seemed Gael had taken offence at his words at their last meeting. And like a damn virus he was determined to corrupt as many of Alejandro's dealings as he could.

He strode into his office as the April sun rose over Lake Michigan. Normally, he stopped to admire the view as he enjoyed his morning espresso. This Monday, however, he tossed his car keys on his desk, tugged off his jacket and went to work.

By 9:00 a.m. he had definite confirmation that it was indeed Gael meddling with the Japanese deal.

He sat back in his chair, fingers tented together as he forced down the acid bite of distaste. Gael's company, Toredo Inc., had grown into an e-commerce powerhouse second only to Alejandro's own company. Not for a single moment had that reality fazed him. His company was worth billions, and more than held its own in the industry. At times when he felt generous, he even welcomed Toredo's competition.

Not this time. Bagging this deal would launch SNV into an echelon of its own. It would be the culmination of the success he'd striven for since walking away from the tatters of what the common man termed a family. Others might accommodate such failures. He didn't. He'd cut his losses on an irredeemable life because nothing he did could fix what was permanently broken. Instead he'd concentrated on what he was successful at. He'd made his first million at twenty-four, just before he left California. In the ten years since, he'd risen to the top. The Ishikawa deal would be his crowning glory. He'd worked too long and hard to see it dismantled by Gael.

His strategy team had suggested hiring a PR company experienced in dealing with Japanese companies to work alongside his in-house PR department. Alejandro had shelved the idea until negotiations had stalled. Although he still had his doubts as to the efficacy of employing an outside PR company, he opened the first file.

The headshot caught his attention immediately, although, staring at the picture critically, Alejandro couldn't pinpoint why. Her mouth was too wide and full, her nose a little too perfectly pointed. Her almond-shaped hazel-gold eyes held too many shadows, and, for his taste, she was wearing a little too much make-up; he preferred the natural look. The shadows and the make-up alone jarred him further into memories he didn't want to dwell on. Like the memories of his brother, they were reminiscent of a past he'd striven hard to forget.

Yet he couldn't drag his gaze away from Elise Jameson's picture. The almost absurd notion that if he stared for long enough the image would come to life gripped him. His gaze dropped past her jaw and neck and he experienced the tiniest stab of regret that there wasn't more to see.

Gritting his teeth, he perused her academic accomplishments, which were impressive enough to compel him to read on. The discovery that Jameson PR was a family company brought a twisted smile, but Alejandro suppressed the useless threat of emotion. Not every family was as dysfunctional as the one he'd left behind.

Suficiente!

He needed his head screwed on straight to see this merger through, not spend time dwelling on the past. He moved on to the other two files. Within minutes he'd dismissed the other candidates.

When he found himself staring at the headshot again, he reached for the phone.

'Margo, set up an interview with the Jameson PR people for this afternoon, would you?'

'Umm, one of their executives is already here. Shall I send her in? Your diary is free since you've cleared most of your appointments already.'

He frowned. 'They came here on the off chance I'd want to see them?' Alejandro wasn't sure whether to applaud them for their brazenness or condemn them for wasting valuable man hours on the likelihood of being hired by SNV.

'Wendell thought it might be prudent in case you wanted to move quickly on the PR front.'

Alejandro made a mental note to increase his team leader's bonus. His gaze dropped to the headshot. 'Which representative from Jameson is here?'

'It's a junior executive—Elise Jameson. I can arrange for a senior member to come in if you pref—'

'No, it's fine. Send her in.' He would glean as much from the younger Jameson as he would from her parents. Besides, he didn't have time to waste. 'I'd like some fresh coffee, too. *Gracias.*'

A brisk knock on the door a few minutes later brought his head up.

Margo entered first, wheeling in a tray of coffee. Alejandro's gaze swung past her, his attention almost compelled to focus on the dark-haired woman who followed. A part of him disliked the fizz of compulsion almost as much as it anticipated his first glimpse of her.

True, his wholehearted immersion in this potential merger had left little time for physical dalliances for the better part of a year now. The occasions when he'd been tempted to indulge in carnal pleasures, the chase had surprisingly grown boring. Enough to abandon his date at the after-dinner-coffee stage on more than one occasion. Nevertheless, he was a red-blooded male, as the momentary tightening in his groin informed him now when Elise Jameson stepped into the office.

The early morning sun struck her face as she paused on the threshold, bringing every feature in her photo to vivid life. Her face was impeccably made-up, just like in her headshot, but where he'd been healthily captivated before by the glossy two-dimensional version, he was paralysingly riveted by the flesh and blood reality.

She advanced farther into the room. Her stride was confident but minimised by the navy pencil skirt whose matching jacket was secured by a single button beneath a full chest. The cut of her clothes immediately drew Alejandro's gaze to her Venus-like body and shapely legs. Attractive. Alluring. But nothing extraordinary.

And then she smiled at a departing Margo, and realisation struck.

Elise bore an unsettling resemblance to a painting he'd once seen hanging in his father's study when he was fourteen years old. The woman had been standing before a window with the sun shining on her arresting features. Her dark hair had been caught at the back of her head, her eyes shut and her face lifted in sun worship. The artist had captured her image from the point of view of a lover staring down at his paramour.

Their differences in height once Elise Jameson reached his desk were strikingly similar.

Except that woman had been nude.

And that painting had also caused prolonged rows between his mother and father, with one vowing to burn the painting and the other mocking the jealous fit. The painting had lasted six days before it'd disappeared. And even though he'd snuck into his father's study to stare at it, Alejandro had been glad once it was gone.

All he'd cared about was that the rowing had ceased. Albeit, inevitably, temporarily.

He blinked the memory away, irritated with his ongoing traipse down memory lane, to find a manicured hand proffered.

'Thank you for seeing me, Mr Aguilar. I'm Elise Jameson.'

He took her hand, noted the soft but firm grip, the smoothness of her skin, the spark that travelled along his palm, and released her.

'I'm aware one of my employees suggested we may be interested in your services, but don't you think it was a touch foolish to just present yourself here? You could've wasted the entire day,' he stated in a voice he knew was clipped.

Her eyes, which were more tilted and vivid in real life, widened a touch, before she blinked back her composure. 'You say foolish, I say impeccably timed,' she replied coolly.

He lifted a brow. 'Are we to disagree so soon? You think that bodes well for our potential working relationship?'

Her shoulders tensed infinitesimally. 'Pardon me for being forward, but if you require a yes-man or -woman who'll jump at your every suggestion, then perhaps Jameson isn't the right fit for you. Sycophancy isn't in our remit.'

He noted then that, although her accent was American, her features bore a hint of an Asian heritage, making her beauty even more enthralling. He also noted his own faint amusement with irritation. Rounding the desk, he approached the tray laden with coffee and bagels and poured his fifth cup of espresso. 'Coffee?'

'No, thank you. I've had my daily allotment. Any more and you'd have to prise me off the ceiling.' One corner of her crimson-painted mouth twitched and Alejandro found his gaze tracing the full curve.

Striding back to his desk, he gulped down half of his beverage. 'In that case, sit down, Miss Jameson, and tell me what *is* in your remit.'

She took the time to unbutton her jacket, giving

him a glimpse of the jade-coloured silk top beneath
and a shadowed cleavage before she sat down.

'Normally, it works the other way round. You tell
me what you need PR-wise and we advise you how
to achieve it, sycophancy not included, of course.'
Another smile that didn't quite reach her eyes.

Over the scent of ground coffee beans, he caught
the faintest hint of her perfume. Crushed berries
mixed with an elusive spice. Unique. Captivating.
He caught himself inhaling deeper to chase the
scent and gritted his teeth.

'We seem to have skipped a step or two in the
traditional interview process, so perhaps we should
go with the flow here.'

She blinked. 'I *could* go with the flow. Except I'm
not even sure where the river starts, Mr Aguilar.
Wendell Grant was equally cryptic when he called
and asked me to come here. Sadly, cryptic won't
cut it if you need my help.'

'Since I haven't decided whether I do or not, I'm
not going to go into the specifics of a highly confidential deal.'

Her mouth tightened a touch before she smiled
her insincere smile. 'If you're worried about confidentiality, our impeccable record speaks for itself.'

'Be that as it may, until you're officially hired, I
prefer to practise a little…restraint.'

Her gaze locked with his for a long moment. Then she nodded. 'As you wish. So let's talk hypotheticals. What can I do for you?'

A frown tugged at Alejandro's brow. She was intelligent. And she was saying all the right things. But he couldn't shake the feeling something else was going on beneath the surface.

'How old are you?' he asked.

Her eyes widened. 'Why is that relevant?'

Alejandro folded his arms, mildly disturbed by his own question. 'Is it a state secret?'

'Of course not.' Her gaze dropped to his desk. 'But you have my file right there in front of you. You've read it so you know my age. If I wanted to lie to you about anything—which I don't, by the way—lying about my age would be the stupidest one to start with, don't you think? And other than to catch me out in a lie, I'm not sure why—'

'Do you always answer a simple question with a diatribe?'

Beneath the make-up, heat flushed her cheeks. Her nostrils flared a touch before she blinked back her composure.

'I'm twenty-five. As it says in my file,' she returned acerbically.

'How long have you worked for your parents?' Again a question he hadn't anticipated asking.

Her mouth compressed. 'Since I graduated university at twenty-one.'

Alejandro studied her silently. To her credit, she didn't fidget.

Unfolding his arms, he rested his elbows on his desk. 'I don't think this is going to work out, Miss Jameson. Thank you for coming.'

First came a look that closely resembled relief. Followed by surprise. Then her lips parted as shock set in. '*Excuse me?*'

'If you can't see your way through answering a few simple questions without getting emotional, I don't see how you can deal with the hard stuff. Margo will see you out.'

She started to get up. Halfway through the act, she dropped back down. 'This is some sort of trick, isn't it?'

It was Alejandro's turn to be surprised. He regained his senses quickly. 'I've been working on a deal that is determined to fall apart at the last minute. Trust me, wasting time with tricks is the very last thing on my mind. Goodbye, Miss Jameson.'

Shadows and questions swirled through her hazel-gold eyes. Her lower lip twisted, as if she was gnawing it from the inside. Eventually she rose, her fingers clamped around her briefcase, her jaw angled with stubborn pride.

Without a word, she turned away from his desk. In that moment, Alejandro wished he'd also turned away. The sight of her trim waist and voluptuous backside triggered another onset of libido-tugging.

He gritted his teeth.

The timing and circumstance of this attraction to her were abhorrent enough to send him to his feet. He'd vowed a very long time ago never to mix business with pleasure when another deal had disintegrated because of a fleeting liaison with a competitor. He'd been young and foolish enough to imagine one would not affect the other. Although the incident had only temporarily slowed down his meteoric rise, Alejandro had learned the lesson well enough to keep his affairs private and brief.

Dragging his gaze from the shapely legs heading for the door, he strode to the window and stared at the view. Lake Michigan didn't offer much solace. Like a lead domino falling over, Elise's image, the feel of their palms touching, the silkiness of her skin, tumbled through his mind. Even the sound of the door shutting barely created a ripple in the sizzling *awareness* gripping him.

What the hell was wrong with him today? First he'd cracked open the vault of memories he'd vowed never to revisit. Now he was getting hot under the collar because of a woman who should barely register on his radar?

He shoved a hand through his hair and turned around.

Elise Jameson was standing before his desk, her eyes square on his.

'Unless I've grown senile in the last five minutes, I'm sure I told you to leave.'

She exhaled slow and steady. Alejandro was certain it was a composure-gaining technique. He had a feeling he'd need one of those before the day ended.

'You did. But I'm still here. The way I see it, you're either going to hire me or we'll never see each other again. So I need to say this. I wasn't being *emotional*. I just didn't see the point of wasting time with questions to which you already had answers. And yes, my…irritation could've been kept on a tighter leash. Give me another chance and you have my word it won't happen again.'

'What *it* are we talking about, just to be certain? The irritation or the emotion?'

The whitening of her knuckles on her briefcase was the only sign that his question had further irked. 'Either. *Both.* Whichever you wish.'

He leaned back in his chair. 'Because I'm the boss?'

'Because you're the boss. Once you hire me. But allow me to say one last thing before you make up your mind.'

'Yes?'

'I'm good at my job. You'll get nothing but the best from me. I promise.'

He shrugged. 'That's a good speech. But it's *just* a speech. I also don't deal in promises.' Promises were easy to make and easier to break. He'd learnt that lesson with shocking frequency as a child.

Her gaze swept down for an instant before rising again. 'Finish the interview. Whichever way you want. Then make up your mind.'

The urge to dismiss her was strong. The urge to have her stay was stronger. Alejandro stepped back from examining why. This whole day had been askew from the start.

'Very well. Sit down, Miss Jameson. But let me make one thing clear.'

She sat back down. 'Yes?'

'I never play tricks. I abhor subterfuge of any kind. Remember that before we go any further.'

She nodded and folded her hands in her lap. 'Understood.'

CHAPTER TWO

WHAT THE HELL just happened?

Elise reeled as if she'd just been dragged upside down through an earthquake. Only she wasn't sure whether she'd survived it or whether what felt like aftershocks were, in fact, another larger quake poised on the horizon, ready to flatten her.

She took another slow, steadying breath.

It was clear the man across the desk from her—the intensely masculine man, whose green eyes tracked her every movement like a spotlight searching for a flaw—was intent on rattling her. Why, she wasn't exactly sure. She was here to help, after all.

Perhaps it was the air of mistrust fairly vibrating off him. Or her own blaring instincts about being in a predator's presence that had produced his thunderous frown when she'd walked in.

Whatever it was, it'd ruffled her calm, which had in turn reminded her of the hell letting her guard down with a client had created just one short year ago.

Her palms grew clammy.

Reeling herself back in, she pushed the disquieting memories away.

Unlike last year, she'd chosen this commission herself. Alejandro Aguilar the man was an unknown quantity, but as CEO his reputation was stellar. She needed to bring her A-game because she couldn't lose this commission.

Earning SNV's contract would mean freedom from Jameson and her parents' clutches. It was the visceral need for freedom that had eroded the temporary relief to be free of this man's disturbing aura when he'd asked her to leave. It was what had halted her flight when every instinct had screamed at her to accept his cold, terse dismissal. And run.

The instinct still clamoured. But then so did the burning need to fulfil her duties to her parents and finally, *finally* walk away.

'I understand completely,' she reiterated, projecting a firmer voice.

'Good. Now answer me this. Hypothetically, if a deal you were working on for a year suddenly started to fall apart, what would you attribute it to?' he asked in that smooth, deep voice that transmitted right through to the soles of her feet.

'That depends on who the other party is, although most eleventh-hour setbacks usually involve money.'

'This one isn't money related. I'm sure of it.' A grim smile fleeted over his lips before his face hardened into a beautifully arresting sculpture she had a hard time dragging her eyes from.

In truth, everything about Alejandro Aguilar was insanely absorbing. From the square-cut jaw to the cheekbones that belonged on a Roman statue, to the broad shoulders, tapered torso and neat backside she'd glimpsed when she'd turned around mid-flight, his looks and aura were overwhelming enough to cause another shaky exhalation.

Silently, intensely, she repeated her warning mantra to herself.

Looks *were* deceiving; power and arrogant charm were stepping stones dangerous men used on their prey. Quite apart from her parents wielding those assets with almost lethal force, her own harrowing experience had taught her to be extremely wary of those qualities.

Marsha and Ralph Jameson had taken turns drilling into their only child that exploiting those elements were what would get her ahead in life. They hadn't accommodated the notion that she wanted to live a different life. Had gone as far as to push her into a situation she'd barely been able to escape from unscathed, then derided her ordeal.

That, above everything her parents had subjected her to, still had the power to burn her raw.

Elise pushed the traumatic memory away and re-doubled her efforts to focus. 'If it's not money, then it's a competitor.' He regarded her steadily. 'But then you know that, too.'

He nodded. 'Yes.'

'So, the question is, what's your competitor offering them that you're not?'

'Nothing,' came the immediate, rigid reply.

'Are you sure?'

One sculpted eyebrow rose. 'Are you questioning the veracity of my due diligence?'

He was touchy. Extremely. Men like Alejandro Aguilar didn't rise to lofty CEO positions of extremely successful corporations by being touchy. Men like him usually had rhinoceros-thick skins. Had she adversely demonstrated her wariness about being in the presence of another powerful man? Was she being overly sensitive?

The tense conversation she'd had with her mother before coming here had put her on edge. Marsha Jameson had wanted to spearhead the SNV commission herself, despite Elise having cultivated the initial contact with SNV's PR department. Elise had stood her ground, a fact that hadn't pleased her mother. It was another reason Elise had stopped herself from walking out of the door just now.

She wouldn't...*couldn't* blow it.

Inhaling slowly, she picked her way through the mine-infested landscape. 'Of course not. But there's nothing wrong with an extra pair of eyes.' For some reason her statement brought an even deeper scrutiny of her face, his gaze holding hers with fierce control. She hastened to continue. 'It *is* why you're looking to hire an outside PR firm, isn't it?'

He remained silent for a brief spell, his fingertips pressed together. 'Your file says you specialise in US–Japanese commissions.'

'Yes.'

'This merger involves a Japanese company.' He paused. 'The Ishikawa Corporation.'

Elise's heart missed a beat. The reason behind it was puzzling. It'd come sooner than expected, but he would've needed to trust her with *some* details in order to secure her help. That he'd done so mere minutes into the interview shouldn't trigger such a response from her.

Yet the tiniest sliver of warmth curled through her.

To counteract it, she nodded briskly. 'Give me an hour to do a little research...I mean a more *per-*

sonal research, and I'll see if I can come up with something.'

His eyes narrowed. 'You think an hour is all it'll take to fix my problem?' he taunted.

'I won't know until I try whether or not I can help you, Mr Aguilar. Let me try.'

'You have half an hour.' He nodded to the far side of his office, where two stylish studded leather sofas faced each other across a smoked-glass coffee table. 'I'll have Margo set you up with a laptop—'

'There's no need. I brought my own.' Elise held up her briefcase and attempted a cool smile.

His scowl deepened. 'I'd prefer it if those confidential details we spoke about don't leave my building. Pass the test, and we'll see about redressing your security access.'

The warmth evaporated. 'Oh, right.' She was irritated with herself for feeling stung by the implication that she wasn't trustworthy. But then hadn't she experienced a similar feeling towards him moments ago? Wasn't she even now kicking herself for continuing to be mesmerised by the sheer depths of raw sensuality oozing from him?

'Is that going to be a problem?' he enquired.

Realising she'd been staring at him for a fistful of heartbeats, she pinned on another smile and rose. 'Of course not. I'm ready when you are.' She headed for the sofa to the sound of Margo being summoned, but the tingle between her shoulder blades and down her back indicated he was watching her. Keeping her movements fluid, she set her case down and removed her jacket before choosing the seat farthest from his desk.

Only then did she risk another glance in his direction.

His head was bent over a document, two fingers tracing the words downward as he speed-read. As with everything she'd noticed about him so far, the action was unmistakably absorbing. To the point where she was in danger of appearing like a hormone-engorged groupie at a rock concert!

She exhaled in relief when Margo knocked and entered. The laptop she set before Elise looked custom-made and top of the line.

After she departed, Elise opened it and stared down at the wallpaper that depicted the majestic Sierra Nevada mountain range in Spain. In the middle of the screen, the SNV logo blinked its request.

'Is there a problem?' Alejandro asked coolly.

'Yes. This requires a password.'

He rose with smooth animal grace, document in one hand and his tiny espresso cup in the other. Pausing at the tray, he refilled his cup, then crossed the room to her.

The notion that she'd unwittingly invited him closer sent equal amounts of chagrin and wariness coursing through her. Her senses jumped as he reached for the laptop. Elegant fingers flew over the keyboard and then he handed it back.

Expecting him to return to his desk, she stared dry-mouthed as he picked up the document and cup, relaxed against the sofa, and crossed one leg over the other.

Elise had always thought that men who sat that way were a little too in touch with their feminine side, but there was nothing even remotely feminine about Alejandro Aguilar as he lounged with almost predatory indolence and flicked through the papers in his hand.

'Unless you intend to prise your answers from my subconscious, I suggest you get on with it, Miss Jameson.'

Heat flared into her cheeks for the third time in less than an hour, eliciting a thorough self-loathing for her inability to curb her jumpy reactions.

Dragging her focus back to the laptop, she settled it on her lap and went to work. Her initial searches produced run-of-the-mill information about the Ishikawa Corporation Alejandro most likely already possessed. She sent three quick emails to trusted sources in Kyoto and Osaka, delved deeper

into the company history, then traced the geneal-
ogy of the founders.

Fifteen minutes later, a tiny spurt of excitement
lanced her.

'Found something you want to share?'

She looked up and found laser eyes trained on
her. 'What?'

'You just made the universal feminine sound of
excitement,' he drawled, lifting his cup and drain-
ing it.

She tried to look away, but found herself unable
to. 'I'm not sure what that is, but yes, I may have
found something.'

'And?' he pressed impatiently.

With effort, she refocused on the screen. 'And I
have another thirteen minutes until my time is up.
So if you don't mind?'

He made a sound beneath his breath, a cross between a growl and a huff, as he stood to refill his
cup yet again. The sound rumbled along her nerve
endings, causing her fingers to stumble over the
keys.

God. What on earth was wrong with her?

Even before the incident that still had the power
to make her stomach turn in sick horror, she'd never
reacted this strongly to another man. Ever. She
hadn't allowed herself to even indulge in thoughts

of the opposite sex since the incident. Sure, there hadn't been a shortage of male attention despite her often blatant lack of interest. From those who wanted to date the boss's daughter to further their own ends, to those who thought she would be accommodating with her affections because of the rumours surrounding her parents' marriage. Each and every one of them had been firmly rebuffed.

Alejandro Aguilar hadn't so much as flicked an interested eyelash in her direction. Yet her senses seemed poised on the edge of an unknown precipice, anticipating a sensation she couldn't quite name.

The ping of an incoming email brought blessed refocusing. She read it quickly, then reached for her phone. 'I need to make a quick phone call.'

'Why?' he asked without lifting his gaze from his document.

'I want to confirm a few things before I present my findings. I still have five minutes left.'

He nodded to the state-of-the-art gadget crouched in the middle of the coffee table. 'Use that phone.'

The bite of distaste stung deeper, prompting her to utter words she would've been better off stemming. 'Are your trust issues as big as your caffeine problem?'

Glacial green eyes sliced into her. 'You call them

problems, I think of them as necessary tools that keep me at the top of my game. Your time is almost up. Use the phone or cut your losses and leave.'

Her hand tightened around her phone. 'You'd toss me out before you hear what I've found out? Just because I state a few home truths?'

'We met an hour ago. Are you naive enough to demand that I trust you in so short a time?'

'Of course not. Nevertheless, I don't appreciate being treated as if I've committed a crime or I'm about to commit one when all I'm trying to do is to help you.'

'You take pleasure in debating non-issues when the only thing that should be important here is your service to me. Learning to give me what I want will go a long way to improving your chances of earning this contract.'

Her breath hitched as another voice surged into her head.

Stop playing so hard to get. Give me what I want and I'll reward you...

The distaste of bitter memories made her snap, 'I told you, if you're looking for someone to lie down for you to walk all over, then I'm the wrong person for the job.'

He strolled the last few steps to the coffee table and dropped his papers on the gleaming surface.

Regarding her with cold detachment, he drawled, 'Lying down, in any shape or form, won't be necessary. But once again we're at an impasse, it seems. The next move is yours.'

Every atom in her body screamed at Elise to slam shut the laptop, get her things, and leave. She stayed put. Tried to get herself under control.

Yes, Alejandro Aguilar had done nothing but make demands that chafed, but they weren't uncommon.

Sucking in a breath that didn't quite rebalance her equilibrium, she set her phone on the table and, using Alejandro's conference set, dialled the number she knew by rote.

When the familiar voice filled the room, Elise wondered for a moment whether she'd done the right thing.

'Hi, Grandma.'

A furtive glance at Alejandro showed both eyebrows lifted in cold mockery.

'Elise, my dear, what a pleasant surprise. I hope you're calling to tell me you've finally found a young man worthy of your affections? I know half of them are dim-witted and the other half focused on the almighty dollar, but a beautiful, intelligent girl like you is capable of landing the right man. You're not being too picky, are—?'

'No, Grandma, I'm not…I'm calling about something *else*.' Cringing and red-faced, Elise switched to Japanese, her chin lowered to avoid Alejandro's drilling stare. 'Something *work* related.'

'Oh. Okay…'

Elise asked the questions she needed to, then a few more to verify she was on the right track, then quickly ended the call, unwilling to invite her beloved grandmother's laser probing into her non-existent love life.

In the seething silence, she cleared her throat, momentarily gripped by embarrassment.

'In the interest of getting this surreal hour over and done with, can we attempt to get past the fact that you blithely dropped your work to make a *personal* phone call?' Alejandro snapped.

'It…umm…wasn't a personal call. At least not from my end…anyway.' Elise stopped, smoothed her damp palms over her skirt, and tried to form coherent words. 'My grandmother is Japanese. She lives in Hawaii now but she still owns several businesses in Kyoto. I thought she might have insights as to what's stalling your merger.'

Alejandro returned her gaze, narrow-eyed, then took the seat opposite her. Wordlessly, he waited, his powerful arms braced on his knees.

Elise cleared her throat. 'Kenzo Ishikawa, Jason and Nathan's grandfather, started the company.'

'I'm aware of that.'

Elise barely managed to keep her lips from pursing. 'He's old school. Traditional.'

'I know what old school means. Explain yourself better.'

'Kenzo has taken a back seat, but he's still on the board.' At his darker glare, she hurried on. 'The company's been based in Kyoto since it was created. Were you planning on moving any of their factories from Kyoto?'

Alejandro nodded. 'Seventy per cent of them, yes. It'll save millions of dollars in revenue and deliver a faster service if we relocate the factories and warehouses to Europe and the US.'

'That probably doesn't matter to him. Since this is a merger and not a buyout, they'll still be associated with it. Kenzo won't want to see everything he's worked for moved to another continent.'

'So your opinion is that this deal is stalling because of *nostalgia*?'

'Sentimentality can be a strong motivator.'

'I don't have time for sentimentality. Or protracted delays. Sitting back while they grapple with their touchy-feely emotions isn't cost-effective for me.'

'Perhaps it hadn't been a card they felt they could play and win,' she ventured. 'But now they do?'

His jaw clenched. One fist wrapped around the other, then he surged to his feet.

'You know, don't you?' she queried.

'Why the Ishikawas have suddenly gone dewy-eyed? *Sí,* I do,' he breathed.

Elise was certain fire would shoot from his nostrils, so devastating was the rage simmering from him.

But he simply returned to his desk. Slightly dazed, she heard him order Margo to summon his strategy team. Once the instructions were snapped out, he jammed his hands into his pockets and turned to the window. Although his gaze remained fixed on the view of Lake Michigan, Elise sensed his thoughts were very much turned inward.

To the source of the problem she'd just helped him uncover.

She sat, hands in her lap, as minutes crawled by. Finally, irritation snapping at her fraught nerves, she stood and shrugged on her jacket. Buttoning it, she approached him.

'Pardon my interruption of your non-Zen rumination, but does the light bulb I just handed you mean that I'm hired?'

His shoulders stiffened. Slowly he turned and

leaned against the window, his ankles crossed. Elise forced her gaze to remain on his face, not glance down to the thighs bunched against the taut fabric of his trousers.

'*Sí*, I'm inclined to give you the commission.'

She tamped down the absurd fizz of excitement. 'I hear a busload of *buts* in there.'

His eyes gleamed a dangerous, hypnotic green. '*But*…we need to establish a few ground rules.'

'I can live with a few *reasonable* rules.'

His mouth twisted with a parody of a smile. 'I assure you, it'll be in your interest to do so.'

She attempted a smile of her own. 'I'll be the judge of that. So shoot.'

'First, there will be instances when if I say jump, you *will* ask me how high.'

'I don't think—'

'Like now, for instance, when I say if you want to be hired, you'll let me finish speaking before you give in to the urge to interrupt.'

She swallowed hard against the urge to tell him to go to hell and reminded herself why she needed this commission. Practising a woefully inadequate restorative breathing exercise, she forced out a nod.

'Second, are we agreed on the extreme confidentiality of this deal?'

'Yes.'

'So, no more phone calls to Grandma.'

Heat rushed up her neck. 'No more phone calls to Grandma.'

'Good. You'll work from here in my office, full time, until this deal is done.'

'I thought I'd be working alongside your own PR team.'

'They'll be brought in when extra support is needed. Don't worry, you'll be adequately compensated.'

Not seeing any way around that bar refusing, she pressed her lips together and nodded.

'Was that a yes, Miss Jameson? If so, I prefer to hear the word, so there's no misunderstanding.'

She gritted her teeth. 'Yes. It was a *yes.*'

'Perfect. You'll start today. Right now. Margo will escort you to HR and you'll sign the requisite confidentiality papers. If you need lunch, let her know and she'll organise something for you.'

'I'm quite capable of getting my own lunch.'

'This is one of those instances where wasting time on a matter will be considered a breach of your work rules.'

Shock widened her eyes. 'I beg your pardon?'

'Lunch, unless you have specific dietary requirements, is lunch, Miss Jameson. Wasting time arguing about who gets you lunch is counterproductive.'

'I… Are you serious?' she asked, unsure whether to be grossly offended or mildly hysterical.

He jerked his head to a connecting door at the far side of the room. 'There's a Michelin-starred chef employed to prepare and serve whatever dish you desire to my personal dining room. All you need to do is ask.'

Elise was aware the scenario he'd just described would be most professionals' idea of a dream perk. Certainly, her parents would relish the chance to laud such a privilege over their competitors and brag about it to clients.

'I have simple tastes, Mr Aguilar. A sandwich from a bistro is perfectly adequate for me. Besides, taking a few minutes away from the office to walk to said bistro helps my cogitative process.' She took a breath. 'But I concede that you're under time pressures. If the chef isn't offended by making me a sandwich, then I'll be happy to eat in your dining room.'

Another hard non smile twitched his sculpted lips. 'I do believe you've just jumped again, Miss Jameson. Although in a puzzlingly overcomplicated way.' He nodded at his door. 'Don't keep Margo waiting.'

Elise forced fists that had unconsciously curled to loosen. She stared at him as he resumed his seat…

his *throne*…and carried on ruling his kingdom as if he hadn't just swatted her away like an annoying fly.

'Is there something about me that rubs you the wrong way, Mr Aguilar?' she asked, suppressing the part of her that questioned her compulsive need to go head to head with him. She reassured herself it was because she didn't want to be caught by a horribly unpleasant surprise further down the line, the way she had last year. If something swirled beneath Alejandro's forbidding mask, she preferred to uncover it sooner rather than later.

He scrutinised her from head to toe, then back again. Slower. More intensely. Until her whole body tingled from the penetrative stare.

'Are you about to start another argument with me?' he enquired silkily.

She shook her head but stood her ground. 'No. But if there happens to be something bothering you about me, I think we need to address it now, before…' She stopped, unwilling to bring the ugly past to this discussion.

One brow lifted. 'Before?'

She shook her head. 'I don't like surprises, Mr Aguilar. I like working in a fraught environment even less.'

His jaw clenched for an infinitesimal moment,

then he did something unexpected. He pressed two fingers against each temple and rubbed. The sigh he emitted was filled with thick weariness.

'This deal should've been done months ago. I don't mind the challenge of a difficult deal if it's warranted,' he murmured, surprising her further by admitting to being anything other than omnipotent. 'But I'm bored by the games the Ishikawas have suddenly decided they want to play.'

'I don't think—'

Cool green eyes met hers. 'Yes, I know what you think. But I'm bored nevertheless. Boredom makes me…unpredictable.'

He was skimming the real issue behind his acerbic attitude. What she wasn't sure of was whether the real reason, somehow, involved her. Just as she was certain he wouldn't answer if she probed further.

She needed to leave this office. Go find Margo and get the HR papers signed. The earlier she got to work, the quicker her last ever commission for Jameson would be done. Then she could truly put the past behind her.

So why was she picking up a sleek bottle of mineral water from the coffee tray and holding it out to him?

Alejandro looked from the bottle to her face. A

face she willed with everything inside her not to redden *again*.

When he didn't take it, she set it down in front of him. 'Try drinking some of this instead of guzzling down gallons of caffeine. It might ease that tension headache you've got going on.'

He ignored the bottle. 'I don't anticipate adding nursemaid to your list of duties. The ones I have in mind for you will be quite involved. Let's concentrate on those, shall we?'

'Duly noted. You can be assured that if I happen to be around when you're struck by lightning or a murder of crows decide to use you for pecking practice, I'll continue on my merry way.'

The smile that twitched his mouth was a shade warmer than the last one. Elise found herself wondering what a genuine smile from him would look like and abruptly stepped back.

Turn around. Go.

She headed for the door.

'Miss Jameson.'

It wasn't a request. It was an order couched in psuedo-reasonable, even tones.

Keep walking. She took another step.

'*Elise.*'

She froze, the sound of her given name so unbelievably sensual coming from his deep, slightly accented tones, that she couldn't suppress a gasp. She slowly turned around.

He was no longer massaging his temples. But he'd wrenched the top off the water bottle, the tip of it poised an inch from his lips.

'One last thing. My company isn't the place to find your next boyfriend or a husband. As long as you're contracted to work for me, you'll practise a zero-fraternisation policy. I find that petty lawsuits are best avoided that way.'

'Are you speaking from personal experience?' she asked before she could stop herself.

His face tightened into a rigid, forbidding mask. Hell, she'd struck another nerve. God, what was wrong with her?

'That is *not* your concern. Just be sure to let Grandma know you'll be disappointing her for a while longer where potential wedding bells are concerned, would you?'

Elise turned back around, too filled with roiling emotions to trust herself to speak.

Keep walking.

CHAPTER THREE

Is THERE SOMETHING about me that rubs you the wrong way?

Of all the words she could've chosen.

Alejandro snorted, inwardly grimacing at the sexual bent he'd afforded the words. But they wouldn't fade away. Like the headache pounding his temples, each heartbeat flashed an image of Elise Jameson onto his retinas, each one more vivid than the last.

Madre de Dios.

He didn't need to waste time on an attraction his principles wouldn't allow him to act upon.

Now he knew the cause of the stalled merger, he could simply pay Jameson PR for services rendered, plus a generous bonus. He had no doubt that Gael had arrived at the same realisation as he had, but, since negotiations hadn't yet been severed with SNV in favour of Toredo, it was most likely Gael hadn't found a satisfactory way to appease the Ishikawas, either.

With that last puzzle unravelled, he didn't need Elise Jameson.

Except she'd rooted out his problem with a single, albeit unorthodox, phone call, whereas his strategy team had spent weeks trying to unravel the mystery of the stalled negotiations.

Sending her away would save the irritating prickling of his senses whenever she was near. Or he could keep her around as the extra pair of eyes she'd advocated until this deal was in the bag.

He stemmed the need to call HR and retract the contract. He never set rules for his staff he didn't follow himself. Regardless of how looking at Elise Jameson's face and body made certain parts of him stir, his only focus in dealing with her would be this merger.

A pep talk. He was giving himself *a pep talk. Por el amor—*

He tossed the curiously empty water bottle on the tray, having no recollection of drinking it. He refused to believe his easing headache was because of his water intake. Or the unknotting of his muscles because Elise had helped him finally unravel the mystery of his failing deal.

He eyed his phone, the temptation to call Gael out on the games he was playing surging high. But no. First he would see what strategy Elise came up with. Every employee had their uses. He'd found hers. No reason not to see how she fared for a few more days.

Resolutely, he got back to work. Only to find his gaze straying with annoying frequency to the clock on his desk. An hour later, he snatched up the phone.

'Margo, do I not recall paying for an efficient time management seminar recently?'

'Umm…yes. Two months ago.'

'Great. So is there any reason the HR team are taking over an hour to send Miss Jameson back up?'

'Oh, yes, sorry. She called to say Mr Michaels was ordering lunch for the department and that he would be adding her order in so she could eat and get the papers signed at the same time. That's super-efficient, don't you think?'

Alejandro gritted his teeth. *'Exceedingly.'*

'Shall I order your lunch now, sir?' Margo asked.

'No.' He started to lower the phone. *'Gracias,'* he tossed in before slamming down the handset.

He told himself he was irritated because he wanted her working ASAP. Time was of the essence.

So why was he eyeing the door, listening out for the click of high heels?

With a vicious curse, he refocused on the extensive list of products his marketing team needed his approval on before offering it through SNV in the next quarter. He was halfway down it when her laughter echoed through the door.

He knew it was her because the charge through his blood was hauntingly familiar. And thoroughly unwelcome. His PA joined in the laughter, as did a male voice.

Alejandro continued reading. More laughter filtered in.

He didn't recall moving. Or turning the door handle.

'So lunch was great, then?' Margo asked.

'Gosh, yes,' Elise enthused. 'The club sandwich was *amazing*! Thanks for recommending it, Oliver.'

Alejandro watched, unobserved, as Oliver Michaels, his head of HR, delivered a smile that made Alejandro's hackles rise.

'My pleasure. Although it's wickedly sinful, it's more than worth the extra hour at the gym.' He patted his abs.

Elise smiled. The act was slow, measured. A revelation. As if she didn't do it often, so was taking time to draw her companions' attention to the extraordinary gift she was bestowing on them. Alejandro's breath strangled in his throat. He watched Michaels and Margo stare as her smile transformed her face from visually stunning to exquisitely entrancing. 'I call that a win, then.'

Oliver Michaels was the first to recover. 'Uh… yeah. I like to think—'

Alejandro stepped into Margo's office, achieving instant silence. 'If you've quite finished rhapsodising about culinary delights, perhaps we can *all* get back to work?'

Margo's eyes widened; no doubt she was realising what Alejandro's chilled voice represented. With a quick nod, she refocused on her keyboard.

Elise met his gaze, her smile now non-existent, tension in her body as her nostrils flared slightly. Alejandro's gaze dropped to her lips. She'd lost some of her scarlet lipstick since she'd left his office. The result was a softer look that made him imagine what she'd look like after being thoroughly kissed. Those lips would be much plumper than they were now, of course. And she would have more natural colour in her cheeks—

Suficiente!

He redirected his attention to Michaels, who was holding out a folder. 'I brought Elise's contract down for you to countersign—'

'Leave it with Margo.' He glanced pointedly at Elise.

She took a few steps forward, then paused. Looking over her shoulder, she let loose a smaller smile. 'Thanks, Oliver. See you around.'

Michaels jerked out a nervous nod.

Alejandro waited until she stepped into his office, and slammed the door. 'See you around?' he repeated.

She stiffened. 'What?'

'I didn't stammer.'

'No, you didn't.' She sighed. 'You're clearly having a bad day. I get that. But do you really need to drag everyone down just because you're in a mood?'

'Excuse me?' Alejandro bristled.

'On second thought, don't answer that. I'm here. I'm ready to work.' She walked away from him, taking the subtle scent of her perfume with her. After retrieving her briefcase, she stopped in the middle of the room. 'Margo said you haven't assigned a desk for me to use yet?'

'No,' he answered shortly, his mind still fixed on the fact that she hadn't answered his question to his satisfaction.

'Is there one I can use?' she pressed.

He inhaled deeply, dismissing the smile, the exchange. Everything that had happened in the last few hours.

Going to his desk, he grabbed the substantial file that was always within reach. 'Come with me.'

He led her to a side door across the room from where she'd done her work that morning. Throwing it open, he walked to the desk directly opposite from the door. Unlike his office, it was sparsely furnished, the only thing besides the desk and chair was a floor lamp set against the single glass wall. He set the file down.

'You'll work in here. I use this office when I don't want to be disturbed. Margo is excellent at keeping physical intrusions away when I need it, but even I can't resist checking my emails when I'm in the middle of a deal.'

Her smile was tight and false. Alejandro willed himself not to wish for the genuine one he'd caught a brief glimpse of. 'It'll do great, thanks.' She pulled the file towards her. 'Anything in particular you want me to watch out for?'

Alejandro shrugged. 'Read up on the merger. I have a conference call with the Ishikawa brothers tomorrow. You'll sit in on it with me. You wanted to be my extra pair of eyes. My Japanese is adequate but not expert. You can be my eyes *and* ears.'

'Okay.'

She dropped her case on the desk and removed her jacket. The second button of her blouse had come undone. Alejandro shoved his hands into his pockets, irritatingly caught between the need to point it out or ogle the creamy silkiness of her skin.

Several seconds passed.

Elise sat down, opened the file and glanced up. 'Was there something else, Mr Aguilar?'

'Leave the door open. There's no phone or intercom in here. It'll save you having to get up and come to me if you have any questions.'

Her gaze flicked past him to his office. Her eyes widened a touch.

'Yes, I can see you from my desk,' he confirmed.

A whisper of a smile touched her lips. 'I'll resist the urge to chew on my nails or burp loudly, then.'

'That would be very considerate of you, *gracias.*'

Her eyes widened further and Alejandro suppressed a rare smile. He'd lived so long in the States that most people forgot he was of Spanish origin. And more than one past conquest had been enthralled by his occasional lapses into his mother tongue.

'I…I didn't actually mean that, Mr Aguilar. That was just a—'

'Joke? It may not seem that way to you, but I do know what those are. I've occasionally been known to make one or two of them myself.'

One shapely eyebrow lifted. 'But not recently?'

The reminder of why this deal was going sour darkened his mood. 'No, Elise. Not recently.'

'Okay. How's the headache?' she asked, then her forehead twitched, as if she hadn't meant to blurt out the question. Alejandro felt an odd sense of kinship as his own unnerving need for something that had no place in this office threatened to return.

'No longer an issue. Perhaps we can work towards keeping it that way by getting this merger back on track?' he said brusquely.

'Umm…sure,' she murmured, still looking mildly puzzled.

Alejandro returned to his desk, satisfied that control had been established. Not that it'd been too far from his grasp. Granted, this morning's revelations had unsettled him.

But he'd never shied away from a challenge. He wasn't about to start now.

CHAPTER FOUR

ELISE RESISTED THE URGE to glance into the outer office. She'd already done that far too many times. Thankfully, not once had Alejandro looked her way. His focus on his work was absolute enough to induce envy. He'd taken a few phone calls, one of which he'd conducted at the far end of his office in front of the bank of floor-to-ceiling windows.

For one absurd second, Elise had wondered whether the low murmured conversation involved a lover. She'd jumped away from the thought as if physically scalded. It was beyond none of her business, and straying into dangerous territory she knew better than to approach.

Refocusing on her work between those times hadn't been a hardship. The intricacies of the merger were staggering and fascinating. But more importantly, the deal Alejandro was chasing would *create* thousands of jobs. Granted, the merger would also elevate him to top five on the World's Richest list, but he would be helping thousands along the way.

The other thing she'd noted was the mind-bend-

ing scale of philanthropy attached to each year's es-
timated earnings. For each year Alejandro achieved
the target he'd set his company, he planned to donate a share of the company's profit to humanitar-
ian projects.

Elise frowned as she finished the charities sec-
tion. Nothing she'd read so far should make the
Ishikawa Corporation want to do anything other
than bite Alejandro's hand off in their haste to secure the merger. If nothing else, they stood to become instant billionaires.

'You're frowning.'

She stumbled to a halt, realising she'd entered his
office. He was bathed in the mid-afternoon sun, the
contrast of olive skin against the rolled-up sleeves
of his black shirt striking enough to command her
stare. 'Oh…I'm almost done reading the file.'

'And?'

'And the deal…the charity benefits… It's all
amazing.'

'*Amazing* directly contradicts that frown.'

She looked away from him, anxiously noting her
elevated pulse rate, and crossed over to the drinks
tray. 'Well, I expected to find a thread of dissatis-
faction right from the beginning. Something that
would indicate they were unhappy. There's nothing.
I'm just wondering why they chose *now* to throw a

wrench in what was from the very start a once-in-a-lifetime opportunity.'

'My guess is another party is dangling promises they may not be able to keep.'

Elise picked up a bottle of water and traced her finger across the top. 'You guess? Sorry, but you don't strike me as the kind of man who guesses.'

'And have you known many men like me?' he drawled.

She flushed, then cursed herself for being flustered at the deliberate taunt. 'You know what I mean, Mr Aguilar.'

Contemplative eyes probed hers for several seconds. When he held out an imperious hand for water, she picked up another bottle and passed it to him, curbing the urge to roll her eyes.

'You're right. I don't guess.'

Surprise spiked through her. 'So you know who's trying to jinx the deal?'

'*Sí*, I do,' he murmured in a tone that sent a shiver down her spine. When he didn't elaborate, she frowned.

'Are you going to tell me who it is?'

'Have you finished reading the report?'

'Not yet.'

He uncapped the bottle and drained half of it in greedy gulps. Elise stopped herself from staring at the solid column of his throat. Or at the dark stubble that had crept over his jaw in the last few hours.

'Go finish it. The "who" doesn't really matter. What I need is a PR strategy on how we can resolve this problem if they remain intransigent.'

She returned to her office, fully aware there was no point pressing him for more information.

When she next raised her head, the view at her window had changed from day to evening, with lights from the adjacent skyscrapers illuminating the night sky. Her senses jumped when Alejandro filled the doorway.

'You done?' he asked, leaning against the jamb.

Elise nodded, wishing there was something else she could refocus her attention on besides the sleek musculature of Alejandro Aguilar's body.

There's the file. Her work. The reason she was here. She'd signed a contract mere hours ago that had drawn clear lines of boss and employee. While her past experience had borne witness that clients could violate contracts, she had a feeling Alejandro would stick rigidly to his.

But that didn't mean she could drop her guard… or ogle his breathtakingly gorgeous body whenever she was in his presence.

She dragged her focus to the file. 'My opinion hasn't changed. They would have to have been offered something over and above what you're offering. And that's…'

'That's what?' he encouraged.

'That's bordering on financial suicide, unless the other party has unlimited funds. Or are willing to go all out to steal this deal from you.'

His gaze swept downward, veiling his expression. Her senses twitched. She used to think she was a good reader of people. A horrific violation of her trust had robbed her of that last year.

Even so, she knew she'd struck somewhere in the vicinity of a nail.

Alejandro turned around without answering.

Elise rose. 'Am I right? Mr Aguilar, is someone going to extraordinary lengths to see you fail?'

'Alejandro,' he murmured.

'What?'

'If we're to work together, you'll have to call me Alejandro.'

Elise wasn't sure why the thought of repeating his name, even minus that sensual Spanish intonation she had no hope of mimicking, sent a shiver of awareness through her. 'I… Okay.'

'The chef has prepared dinner for us. Come. We'll talk some more while we eat.'

She followed him out of his office to a set of smoked-glass doors, which swung open to reveal a small twelve-seater dining room. At the head of the table and directly adjacent, two places had been set, complete with silver tableware and glasses that indicated this was a multi-course meal.

They sat, and the chef walked in bearing two platters. Elise chose the chicken ravioli starter and almost groaned with pleasure as the delicate tastes melted on her tongue.

'Okay, I take it back. Given the choice of going outside for fresh air and a sandwich or this, I'll choose this every time.'

The chef, who was almost at the door, grinned at her compliment. Smiling in return, she turned back to her place and noticed Alejandro's scowl.

Her smile dimmed. 'Um, in case you missed it, I'm conceding that I was wrong before. No need to give me the evil eye.'

His eyes narrowed on the shutting door before returning to hers. 'Do you make a habit of flirting with every man you come into contact with?'

Elise froze in the act of lifting her fork. 'I *don't* flirt,' she bit out, her insides congealing at the accusation that struck a direct hit and dredged up haunting memories. No matter how many times she'd told herself the assault hadn't been her fault, a part of her always wondered if she'd emitted the very vibes she'd striven to avoid her whole life.

Her parents might have chosen to use their God-given looks and charm as weapons, and Marsha Jameson might have advised Elise to exploit her sexuality to her advantage, but Elise had vowed never to follow in their footsteps.

Unfortunately, that rigid belief had proven to be an irresistible challenge for Brian Grey...

Hastily shoving aside bitter memories, she pushed the chair back and surged to her feet.

Her wrist was captured before she'd taken a single step. 'What do you think you're doing?'

'I don't like the tone of this conversation. Perhaps I was too hasty in taking back the benefits of getting my own meal. *I don't flirt,*' she reiterated, the need to reassure herself that what had happened a year ago hadn't been her fault pumping through her blood. 'But I have manners. And if someone does something nice for me, I *thank* them.'

He regarded her intensely for far too long. 'Sit down, Elise. We're not done.'

She shook her head. 'I've lost my appetite. Besides, it's seven in the evening. I didn't sign up to work all hours.'

'But you committed yourself to working reasonable work hours. Are you calling this an unreasonable hour?'

'I'll re-evaluate if I'm not subjected to unfounded

allegations,' she challenged. She looked pointedly at the hand manacling her wrist.

He waited a beat, then released her. 'You were enjoying your food a few minutes ago. I'll refrain from ruining our meal with...touchy subjects.'

Elise eyed her plate, then the door. She knew her outburst had flared brightly on Alejandro's radar, but walking out at this stage would be counterproductive. She sat back down.

'While you're doing that, perhaps you'd like to remember that I haven't flirted with *you*. Unless you count yourself *above* men?' It was a cheap shot, regretted the moment she uttered the words.

One corner of his mouth quirked. 'We'll leave that debate alone, shall we?'

Her face reddened slightly, and for the rest of the first course they didn't speak.

Once the second course of roast beef and vegetable medley had been served, he held up the bottle of expensive red. 'Wine?'

About to refuse, she sprung for a little Dutch courage to see her through and nodded. 'I'm not much of a wine drinker, or a drinker at all, so don't hold it against me if I don't appreciate the vintage.'

He filled her glass, then his. 'I prefer honesty to a pretentious diatribe on non-existent flavours and bouquets.'

Despite the residual sting of his earlier accusation, a smile tugged at her lips. 'Score one for me.'

Sharp eyes met hers. 'Remain straight with me in all things, and you'll score a lot more.'

For some reason the statement produced equal amounts of dread and anticipation. Anticipation of what, she had no idea. They were halfway through their main course before he spoke again.

'So, in light of what you've discovered, what would Jameson PR advise?'

She knew her parents would advise him to go for the usurper's jugular. Setting a bloodhound on the trail of salacious gossip and secrets to discredit was a favourite tactic her father relished.

'A charm offensive. And a reminder of everything they have to gain by merging with you.'

'Not a declaration of war on my competitor?'

Her mouth soured. 'You can take that route if you want to, I guess.'

'Which route would you take?'

'Not that. Blood and gore turn my stomach.'

'Perhaps you need a stronger disposition,' he mocked.

Choosing not to take the bait, she sipped her wine, a little surprised when it slipped down smoothly. 'The looking-into-the-whites-of-their-eyes approach works, Alejandro. Nothing beats a personal touch. How many times have you met the Ishikawa brothers face to face since deciding to pursue this merger?'

He swirled his wine glass. 'Twice.'

'After you had your team investigate their viability and profit margins?'

'Of course.'

'I'm guessing both times were here in the States where you wined and dined them at the best restaurant in town?'

'Their every wish was catered to. They left happy.'

'In your opinion.'

His gaze probed hers. 'What's your point?'

'I'm willing to bet my sizeable manga collection that you didn't divulge a single personal detail about yourself.'

'At the risk of repeating myself, I don't do—'

'Touchy-feely. Yes, I'm aware. But letting them see you as remotely...*human* may have prevented this from happening.'

'That might work for the average Mom and Pop ice-cream-parlour business. If they can't see their way past those...*feelings* to a multibillion-dollar merger, then perhaps I'm dealing with the wrong business.'

She sent him a droll look. 'We both know this

isn't a mistake. The Ishikawa Corporation's business record is outstanding. So is SNV's. A successful merger would be the stuff of breaking news headlines and serious accolades. All you'll need to do is…bend a little.'

'Is that what you'd do in my shoes? Bare your life to strangers in order to secure a deal?'

She lifted her glass and took a healthy gulp, relishing the warmth that blanketed her insides. 'We're not talking about me here.'

'You're fond of hypotheticals. So let's have it. Would you give yourself the same advice, were you in my position?'

'Maybe.' She bore his intense scrutiny for a minute before she sighed. 'Yes, I would.'

'And what would you tell them about yourself?'

Elise shook her head. 'That's too broad a question.'

'Let's streamline, then. You attended a university on the west coast when your family is based in a state with excellent universities. Why?'

Nerves began to eat into the warmth. She took another sip, despite the faint warning that this form of Dutch courage hadn't been her best idea. 'The need to broaden my horizons?'

'If you had such a need, why did you return to work with your parents?'

She stiffened at the other raw subject that grated her nerves. 'Is there a law against that?'

'Is that the answer you'd give a prospective business partner?'

'No…' She paused, aware she had skidded towards a chasm of her own making. 'I agreed to work at Jameson in return for my parents paying for my university tuition.'

A slow frown gathered on his brow. 'They expected you to pay for the education they gave you?'

Elise chose to blame the Malbec for loosening the tight leash she normally had on her emotions. 'They expect a lot of things. Including not giving free rides to anyone, including their daughter.'

The enlightened gleam in his eyes further unnerved her. 'Things aren't cordial between you and your parents?'

A harsh laugh escaped before she could stop it. 'You could say that.'

'Then why do you work with them?' he queried.

'Because jobs don't automatically fall from the heavens the moment you graduate from college. And if, by some divine grace, you make it to a second or third interview and your prospective boss finds out that you're the daughter of Marsha and Ralph Jameson, they question why you'd snub the chance to work for the exalted Jamesons. Half of them won't touch you because they don't believe you'll be committed to your job. The other half have certain…preconceived notions about you and won't even give you a chance. Seven months of polite rejections and my parents demanding repayment of their loan left me little choice.'

Elise took another sip of wine to drown the sinking knowledge that she'd divulged far more than she'd intended to.

Silence seething with questions filled the room. Alejandro levelled a gaze at her, speculation swirling in his shrewd eyes. 'And is that debt paid off?'

She swallowed. 'No. But I'm almost there.'

He raised his brow. 'Almost?'

'Yep. With your help, of course.'

'My help?' he enquired thinly.

'Helping you nail this deal would be great for you, of course, and it'll boost my résumé, too, but, more importantly, it'll see me freed from the shackles of Mum and Dad. So really, it's a trifecta of pure *winning.*'

Alejandro slowly swirled his glass. 'I see.'

Shame nibbled at her. As he continued to stare at her, heat that had nothing to do with the great food and wine swarmed up her neck. 'I'm sorry, you didn't ask for my life history.' Setting the nearly empty glass down, she stood. And swayed. Alejandro surged up and grasped her waist. She averted her gaze from eyes that saw way too much. 'I told you I wasn't much of a drinker.'

'*Sí*, you did, but you're not drunk. Trust me, I know the difference.' His voice was faintly self-mocking.

'All the same, this isn't going to look good in the morning, is it?' she muttered.

'You barely finished your glass. I'm not going to hold it against you.'

Her eyes flicked to his. And stayed, absorbed by the faint gold flecks splaying from his pupils. 'Thanks,' she whispered.

'*De nada,*' he murmured.

They remained like that, their breaths close enough to mingle. Elise knew it was unsafe to let those dark-rimmed eyes bore right into her soul. 'I didn't mean to carry on. I just…'

His eyebrow lifted. 'You just…?'

'I don't like talking about my parents.'

'Why?'

'It…it just hurts too much, you know?'

A curiously bleak smile quirked his lips. 'No. I don't know.'

Elise frowned. 'Of course not. I'm guessing you had a brilliant childhood, filled with nauseatingly blissful memories.'

The hands curled at her waist tightened impercep-tibly. 'Nauseating more often than not, yes. Bliss-ful, no.'

Her brain suddenly locked onto the fact that his hands were on her body. Elise couldn't think be-yond the electric heat seeping into her skin. Or the need to feel it glide elsewhere.

'Well, I'm sorry.'

'For what?'

She attempted a shrug. 'For both of us.'

'I don't need your pity.' His voice was edgy, filled with a thousand barbs.

She shivered. Immediately, his hands slid up her arms, warming her. Elise struggled to focus. 'I wasn't offering it. I was just...'

His gaze dropped to her mouth and her thoughts momentarily scattered. Dragging her eyes from his face restored temporary sanity. A question that had been probing the back of her mind surged forward, but his hands on her body wreaked havoc with her thought processes.

'Alejandro?'

'Sí?' he breathed.

Her insides shook at the sultry, exotic word. 'You can let me go now. I promise I won't fall over.'

His hands tightened on her for a heated second,

then he freed her. 'Good to know. Would you like some coffee or shall we put an end to this *work*day?'

She gripped her arms where his had been a moment ago, absurdly aware she wasn't ready for the evening to end. 'You were going to tell me who was behind the stalled merger.'

Several emotions curled through his eyes, most of them forbidding enough to send a chill through her.

'It's my brother,' he finally offered. Contrary to the expression in his eyes, his voice was bled of every emotion.

'Your *brother*?'

'Yes.'

'But…why?'

He took a step back, then another. Striding to the ever-present coffee cart, he poured a shot of espresso. 'Because like you, for me, *family* isn't a word that conjures hearts and flowers.'

Elise wished she didn't understand what he meant. All the same… 'That's still a little extreme, isn't it? Your brother wants to hurt you that much?'

His mouth twisted. 'You assume I'm capable of being *hurt*. At the worst, he'll make a nuisance of himself. No more.'

The staggering confidence behind the words further chilled her. And yet, she felt an affinity with

Alejandro, sensed an underlying emotion that she couldn't quite pinpoint.

She was twisting the puzzle in her mind when he drained his cup and set it down. 'I think I've used up my reasonable workday quota where you're concerned. Come.'

He walked out of the dining room. She followed at a slower pace, and entered his office to find him returning from hers with her jacket and briefcase.

He held out her jacket for her, and Elise murmured her thanks. About to bid him goodnight and beat a hasty retreat, she froze as he caught up his own jacket and came towards her. 'You're leaving, too?'

'I'm taking you home.'

She shook her head. 'There's no need to do that. The subway will get me home in twenty minutes.'

He took her elbow and steered her towards the door. 'It's late. Letting you brave the subway at this time of night is out of the question. If nothing else, I wish to see you return to work tomorrow in one piece.'

'It's really not—'

'You haven't already forgotten our agreement to dispense with unnecessary arguments, have you?'

She firmed her mouth and followed him into what looked like a private lift. Enclosed in the small space, she couldn't think of one thing to say to the man whose presence loomed powerful and vibrant beside her. In contrast, she felt small and shamefully inept, so she turned her face away from him. To the mirror that reflected his image in perfect detail.

Even in profile, Alejandro was unforgivingly captivating. In the harsh light, his skin glowed a vibrant olive, his thick dark hair gleaming invitingly. Elise had never felt the urge to touch a man's face, let alone his hair. Pursuing a double major had been time-consuming enough, and the casual dates she'd occasionally accepted in college ended when she discovered sex was the subtext behind each date.

That reality had followed her into her working life, but she'd become an expert at holding male interest at bay.

But staring at Alejandro, she felt an alien need to do the opposite, to give in to the subtext of sex pulsing through her right to the tips of her fingers.

As if he sensed her unvarnished scrutiny, Alejandro's head snapped up. Their eyes met in the mirror. His gaze held hers easily, compelling her completely, so she couldn't look away. The whine of the descending lift the only sound, they stared at each other as silence seethed, thickened into something else. Something that had intense heat dredging low in her belly, and flaring tingles all over her body.

His gaze probed, darkened with each jagged second. It dropped to her lips, and Elise, as if she were under a spell, parted them.

Someone made a sound. A tiny fracture of breath. The beginning of a curse. Or a prayer. She never got the chance to guess.

The lift arrived with a slight bump and the doors glided open.

And the spell was broken.

CHAPTER FIVE

ELISE HAD RIDDEN in her fair share of supercars, her father being a firm believer that a show of power and success bred even more of the same. Each time she'd ridden with her father, she'd prayed for the ride to be over as quickly as possible, silently enduring the 'life lesson' speeches that came with those trips, while Ralph Jameson had walked away congratulating himself for showing his daughter what material benefits could be plucked like fruit from the nearest low-hanging tree, should she play her cards right.

Tonight, she was far from uninterested. Her gaze strayed frequently to the man behind the wheel of the Bugatti, a tiny part of her not minding the traffic that slowed their progress through downtown Chicago.

Even the silence, although charged with residual awareness from the lift, was welcome. It gave her a chance to breathe, and evaluate just what it was about Alejandro Aguilar that threatened the careful foundations of the walls she'd built around her emotions and sexuality.

When it came right down to it, he'd done nothing presumptive or offensive to make her believe she had anything to fear from him. His comment about her flirting had stung, of course, but he'd dropped the subject at her challenge. Which was far more than a few of the men she'd interacted with professionally and privately had done in the past.

But that tiny consideration still didn't account for why she felt this unsettling excitement just by being next to Alejandro Aguilar.

Whatever it was, she needed to get it under control quickly.

He changed lanes as they neared her South Shore apartment. In an effort not to stare at his hands or the taut thighs centimetres from hers, or even breathe in the aftershave-mingled maleness of him, she cleared her throat.

'So…are you going to go after your brother?'

His jaw clenched as he pulled to a stop at a traffic light. One hand rested on the top of the steering wheel, the other scrubbing restively over his stubble. 'No. For now, I'm choosing to resist that impulse.'

A breath freed itself from her chest. 'I'm glad.'

He glanced at her before he eased away at the green light. 'Do you advocate the "make love, not war" route with all your clients?'

'My commissions so far have involved damage limitation or using the best PR approach that makes the client look good. I won't be helping you if I advocate an approach that makes you look bad to investors in the long run.'

He slid another glance at her. 'What do you care? This is your last commission. What happens after this shouldn't concern you.'

Elise bit her lip as a mildly hollow sensation washed over her. 'No, I guess it shouldn't. Maybe I don't want my swan song to leave a bad taste in my mouth,' she replied. She looked out of her window and saw her apartment block slide into view. She indicated the quieter side street. 'If you pull over here, I'll jump out.'

He ignored her and the no-parking zone in front of her building and stopped before the double glass doors. Stepping out, he came round and opened her door.

Elise took a gulp of restorative fresh air. 'Thanks for the ride.'

He took her arm and started towards the double doors. 'You can thank me by letting me see you to your door. You can also tell me why your building doesn't have a doorman. Or adequate security.' He eyed the hippy-looking couple who breezed out, then transferred his scathing gaze to the doors that didn't quite shut behind them.

To counteract what the thought of being enclosed with him in another lift was doing to her insides, she waved his terse demand away. 'I have a super. Does that satisfy you?'

'No, it does not.'

Her mouth twisted. 'Not everyone can afford a Barrington Hills mansion, Alejandro.'

He pressed the lift button. When it didn't arrive quickly enough, he pressed it again, several times. 'I don't live in Barrington Hills.'

'My parents do.'

He stared at her. 'And you choose to live here?'

'Yes,' she answered simply.

He didn't probe further, leaving Elise with the feeling that the subject of family was as unwelcome to him as it was to her. What he did probe was the lift button, uttering a skin-flaying Latin curse when the lift made no move to arrive.

Relief and disappointment spun through her. 'I'll take the stairs. I'm only on the third floor.'

He whirled with fluid grace and indicated for her to precede him. Battling to suppress her self-consciousness, she hurried up the stairs, and arrived at her door two minutes later, struggling not to pant. Alejandro, on the other hand, had barely broken a sweat.

She unlocked her door. Almost reluctantly her eyes drifted up only to find his waiting for her. 'Since conventional working hours are out the window, what time do you need me tomorrow?'

'To avoid another argument, you can arrive at seven.'

Her eyes widened. 'As opposed to what? *Five a.m.?*'

He shrugged. 'That's when my work day starts.'

'Dare I ask when it ends?'

'When the coffee machine threatens to quit. Which it does on a daily basis.'

She laughed. His lips twitched. Then his gaze dropped to her mouth.

The laughter died. She scrambled backwards, bumping her backside into the door. 'I'll see you in the morning?'

Penetrating eyes collided with hers. '*Sí.* You will. *Buenas noches.*'

He departed with the quiet strength and power of a jungle predator. And even though his footsteps barely echoed down the stairs, she found herself listening for them.

Catching herself, she stepped back and shut her door.

Twenty minutes later she was showered and

dressed in her favourite sleeping shirt. Sitting in bed, she tugged her laptop close and powered it on. Her buzz disappeared beneath the volume of emails from her mother earlier in the day, then her father demanding responses to her mother's emails.

She'd muted her phone for her interview with Alejandro and then neglected to turn it back on. She activated the sound and wasn't at all surprised when the handset rang almost instantly.

The buzz now replaced with cold trepidation, she braced herself and answered the call.

'Finally! Your father and I were beginning to wonder whether you'd been abducted by aliens,' her mother snapped, her voice containing a bite that always raised Elise's hackles.

'I turned the sound on my phone off when I met with Mr Aguilar. Things got out of hand after that.' She immediately cringed at the poor choice of words.

She didn't bother retracting them, because her mother was already enquiring sharply, 'Out of hand? Are you saying we didn't get it? Damn, I should've handled it myself. But we're the number one PR firm in Chicago. People beg to come to us, not the other way round. All the same, this commission could've been huge for us. You should've called us when things started going bad. Ralph! Come here. We have a problem.'

Elise's grip tightened on the phone, all too familiar anger and hurt welling inside her. 'Mom—'

'Your father and I will have to see if there's any way to salvage it—'

'Mom!'

'What?'

'I signed the agreement with SNV this afternoon.'

Stunned silence followed. Elise tried to breathe through the hurt clogging in her chest.

'Well, that's…commendable?'

The question mark hooked like a rusty claw into her. It was the same question mark with which they'd greeted her devastation after being nearly assaulted by a client they'd pushed her into dealing with.

'Are you sure it wasn't a harmless pass, Elise?'

'You're mistaken. Brian Grey doesn't normally go for girls like you…'

She breathed through the anguish. 'Thanks for your rousing belief in me,' she replied, but the murmur of voices in the background told her they were engaged in a side conversation about her.

Her father took over a minute later. 'I hear congratulations are in order?'

Again the insidious disbelief that she'd been able

to land SNV's business. 'Is that a question, Dad?' she asked stiltedly.

'You can take that tone all you want, but you've made it perfectly clear you're just passing through the business that kept you in clothes, ponies, and round-the-world vacations, not to mention college tuition fees.'

'Some of those things were your responsibility to me as my parents. The others I never asked for. And I'm paying you back for my education. Let's not forget that.'

'You wouldn't have had to if you hadn't misled us about your true intentions. We didn't pay hundreds of thousands of dollars to send you to college to study *art*. Any fool can draw. You were supposed to make marketing and PR your main focus.'

'I'm not a fool, Dad. And I graduated with *double* majors. You just choose to ignore that fact because it suits your argument. I'm sorry I disappointed you and Mom by not wanting what you want, but my life is my own. If you can't respect that—'

'Elise—'

Her father was cut off abruptly as her mother took control. 'Enough of this. These arguments give me migraines and I can't afford one tonight. We're entertaining the Greenhills. They're not as prestigious as Alejandro Aguilar, of course, but both your father and I need to be on top of our games. A commission from them will guarantee us a significant mention in the *Tribune*. I know you'd rather be doing other things than talking to us, so just forward me a copy of the contract so Accounts can set up a payment schedule with SNV.'

Elise exhaled shakily. She'd tried to bury the futile wish for affection from them, but their cold-hearted indifference to her and everything except climbing the social and financial ladders, despite the shockingly harrowing events of last year, still caused anguish. 'Mom—'

'Goodbye, Elise.'

Her mother hung up, leaving her no choice but to swallow the words that never quite managed to pave the way for a non-confrontational conversation.

She blinked rapidly when she realised tears were forming. Dashing her hand across her face, she forwarded the contract to her mother.

Powering down her laptop, she slid properly into bed and pulled up the sheets to her chin, firmly refusing to dwell on the past.

Instead, she analysed her day.

In some ways, today could've gone better. She could've summoned more control over her errant emotions around Alejandro, for instance. Been less absorbed by his raw magnetism, that hint of bleakness that echoed the knot trapped inside her.

But she'd secured and held on to the SNV commission.

Tomorrow would be better.

She groaned out loud when her alarm sounded at six. Rolling over, she debated the wisdom of making middle-of-the-night decisions like running to SNV's offices as a perfect start to the new day.

Eyeing the backpack she'd readied with her work clothes and everything she needed for the day, Elise groaned again, wondering what she'd been thinking.

You need a clear head to deal with Alejandro Aguilar. Running does that for you.

Grudgingly accepting the voice of reason, she rose and donned her running gear. Tying her hair into a ponytail, she caught up the backpack and headed out.

Twenty-five sweaty minutes later, she arrived at SNV. She was gulping thirstily from the water fountain when she sensed she was being watched. Her heart leapt into her throat, but when she raised her head it wasn't Alejandro, but a sandy-haired man who approached with a smile and an outstretched hand.

'I'm Wendell Grant. I'm with the strategy team on the Japanese merger. Alejandro mentioned he'd gone with my recommendation and hired you.'

Wondering when Alejandro would've had a chance to do that since it was only six thirty, she plastered a smile on her face. 'Oh, I see. I guess I owe you big for that.'

His smile widened. 'I accept payment in caffeine-related beverages.' He fell into step beside her and held the lift door for her. 'Good thing is, in this place, it's *free*,' he whispered conspiratorially.

Elise laughed. 'Noted.'

He pressed the button for the same floor Alejandro's office was located, then sent a swift glance over her body. 'You better hustle. Alejandro might want a meeting. In my experience it's better to make yourself available and not be needed, than the other way around.'

She nodded brisk thanks, although her body developed a curious thrum at the mention of Alejandro's name as they exited the lift. Wendell turned right and she headed for the women's bathroom that held fully stocked shower cubicles.

'Oh, by the way...'

She paused and turned.

'I take my coffee black with two sugars,' Wendell said.

Acknowledging him with a quick wave, she darted into the bathroom.

She arrived at Margo's desk one minute before seven. The middle-aged PA looked up and rolled her eyes.

'Be warned. He's in a mood. There's a briefing in the conference room. You better head there, too. He'll join you when he's done with his phone call.'

Elise eyed the door, heard the growled imprecation from within, and exchanged a nervous smile with Margo before heading the other way.

She entered the conference room and greeted the three men and three women comprising the strategy team. After Wendell made introductions, Elise went to the coffee cart and prepared two coffees, and held one out to him.

'Black, two sugars.'

He took the coffee from her and took a sip. 'Perfect. You can stay.'

Exaggerated groans and ribbing sounded around the table.

Smiling, Elise started to raise her cup, and froze at the sight of Alejandro, silently observing her from the doorway.

She locked her knees, the bolt to her stomach just from the sight of him enough to knock the breath from her lungs. Tension emanated from him. The team lapsed into silence, furtive glances passing between them.

Alejandro prowled forward and stopped at the head of the table. 'You've all met my new PR guru. Good. This will be a short meeting.'

Bodies shifted. Throats cleared. The tension remained.

'Are you going to sit down, Elise?' Alejandro addressed her without looking her way.

'Uh, sure.'

About to take the seat farthest away, she froze again when Alejandro pointed to the chair adjacent to him. Again without looking her way.

Clutching her untouched coffee, she made her way round the table and slipped into the chair. A few heartbeats later, Alejandro sat down.

Like yesterday, he wore a black shirt and faintly pinstriped tailored trousers. If he'd worn a tie with the ensemble, he'd discarded it—the two top buttons opened to reveal his strong throat and the hint of silky curls. She quickly averted her gaze from the evocative sight and concentrated on the file in front of her. The thin file that, upon closer inspection, held everything she'd discovered yesterday.

Her eyes widened. Had he returned to the office last night to put this together? The man was superhuman.

'Yesterday, Elise confirmed what we've all suspected for the past few days. The Ishikawa Corporation is considering another player for the merger. What the report doesn't say is that player happens to be my brother.'

Elise tensed at the icy chill of his tone as shocked murmurs went around the table.

'Your brother?' Wendell echoed.

Alejandro's eyes hardened a touch. 'Yes. He's CEO of Toredo Inc. That fact shouldn't alter our strategy. At least not yet. Elise believes Kenzo Ishikawa and the proposed relocation of the factories is the bone of contention fuelling the sudden switch in their end goal. We'll concentrate on that instead.'

Wendell frowned and glanced at Elise. 'Their *grandfather*? Are you sure?'

She nodded. 'As sure as I can be without hearing it straight from his mouth.'

Alejandro levelled a hard stare at him. 'Do you have a problem with that assessment? If so, prove it wrong,' he bit out.

Wendell's eyes widened. 'Umm…no, I believe her.'

'Good. I want a preliminary report of what it'll cost to relocate fifty per cent of the factories and leave the remainder in Japan for the next five years. That will be all.'

He rose, signalling an end to the meeting. A few steps from the door, he looked over his shoulder. 'Elise?' Her name was a terse command.

She rose, aware of the speculative glances she drew.

Wordlessly, she followed him into his office, the door swinging shut behind them. The familiar-looking coffee cart stood beside the sofas. Alejandro strode to it and poured himself an espresso.

After taking a healthy gulp, he faced her.

'Are popularity contests your thing?' he enquired. His tone would have been cordial, but for the deadly bite threading it.

Elise frowned. 'What?'

'You walk into a room and instantly feel a burning need to make sure everyone *likes* you, is that it?'

A quiver of anger, and something else she couldn't define, shot through her. 'The only thing I'm sure of right now is that I have *no* clue what you're talking about. Wait, maybe I am sure of one thing. You definitely woke up on the wrong side of the bed.'

His mouth twisted. 'You're assuming I went to bed at all.'

'Well then, that's your problem right there. Grumpiness due to sleep deprivation is a common ailment. And I don't need you to fight my battles for me.'

'Excuse me?'

'I could've defended my findings to Wendell. You didn't need to lumber in.'

Green eyes narrowed. 'Watch it, Elise. You're in danger of forgetting who's boss.'

Another shiver passed through her, but it was in response to the sparks arcing through the air. And the fact that she wasn't shying away as she'd promised herself last night she would. In truth, the opposite seemed to be the case. Something inside her relished it. 'I haven't forgotten. But I appear to have done something specifically to annoy you between last night and right now. Something I have no clue about—'

'Unless I haven't been paying attention to my team, Wendell Grant hasn't lost the use of his limbs. Is there any reason you felt the need to fetch him coffee?'

Her snort escaped before she could stop it. 'You're annoyed about *that*?'

His brows clenched in a frown. 'I don't wish to set a precedent,' he snapped. 'Or breed an atmosphere of sexism at the workplace.'

Elise took a deep, bracing breath. 'So why didn't

you just say that? Why go with the popularity angle? And yesterday it was about me *flirting* with Oliver.'

'You're making my point for me.'

'Am I? Or are you going out of your way to find fault with me because *you* have a problem with me?'

His jaw tightened. 'I assure you—'

'No. Let *me* assure you. I'm familiar with a work environment where it's believed that throwing your weight about and reminding those around you who's boss every minute of every day is the way forward. Both times you've bitten my head off, your employees have seemed surprised. Which tells me you don't normally do that. Your problem is with me specifically. So I'll explain myself in the hope we can start another day with a clean slate, shall I? I met Wendell on my way up. He told me he'd recommended you to use Jameson. We joked about what his reward would be. I got him the coffee as a *thank-you*. End of story.' Realising she'd delivered another diatribe, Elise heaved in a breath.

Alejandro stared at her for several beats without speaking. Eyes still fixed on her, he drained his espresso, set down the cup on his desk and prowled to where she stood.

'As I said…you want to be *liked*,' he taunted, her ramble clearly having had zero effect.

'Are you *serious*—?'

'So, what about me?' he inserted. 'Do you *like* me, Elise?'

'I… What?' She exhaled.

He shrugged, piercing green eyes examining her face in rapt detail before they locked on her mouth. 'Grant merely recommended you. There were two other candidates I could've gone for. I chose you. So, tell me? How will you thank *me*?'

Electricity stormed the air. Invisible sparks flew, crackling thick and volatile charges between them. Her mouth tingled, her throat growing dry as she tried to swallow and speak. The first few attempts, words failed her, her senses swimming as she tried to step back from the edge of the dangerous abyss that suddenly loomed before her.

She shook her head. The movement was jerky. Uncoordinated. 'I'm not falling for this,' she said, her voice a croak above a whisper.

'Falling for what, Elise?' he asked, his tone containing an unfamiliar pulse that sent more shivers chasing through her body.

'For whatever trap you're setting for me.'

'You're far too fixated on traps,' he drawled, his gaze still glued to her mouth.

'You're far too adept at laying them.'

'I'm waiting, Elise.'

She licked her lips. It was a quick lick, a desperate act to stop the insane tingling. But his eyes darkened dramatically, and he exhaled a breath that sounded pent-up. Aggravated.

What was happening—?

No. Whatever was happening here didn't require fathoming. She knew first-hand how quickly things could escalate from seemingly tranquil to potentially life-scarring. She'd been wary before Brian Grey had taught her a salutary lesson last year. But that incident had only tripled her efforts to stay away from emotional and sexual pitfalls.

Granted, Alejandro evoked an entirely different sort of apprehension from the sensations Brian Grey had produced in her. But they were all equally dangerous. Even more so this time, because her emotions weren't as non-receptive as they'd been with Brian.

The realisation troubled her enough to propel her one step back. Then another.

Do you like *me, Elise?*

This close, when his scent was sucking her into that sensual vortex, when his body was close enough to feel the heat pulsing off him, her senses screamed *yes*.

'I'm here to work, Mr Aguilar. There's nothing in my contract that says I can't be *nice* to other people. So unless you have another problem with me, or something specific you wish me to work on, I'll be in my office.'

She turned and walked away, painfully aware of his gaze tracking her every step.

Elise entered the room she'd used yesterday and stopped in her tracks. The space had been transformed. A computer had been set up, together with a phone, sleek stationery and her own refreshment trolley. Two large ferns had been placed at each end of the window, and a bouquet of fresh, expensive-looking flowers stood on a pedestal beside her desk.

She looked over her shoulder to find him staring at her. Elise's lips parted with the urge to say something, but, after their terse exchange, appropriate words failed her.

Alejandro turned away from her and the moment passed. Strolling with lean-hipped grace, he took a seat at his desk.

'Your brief today is to find me an in to Kenzo Ishikawa,' he ordered.

Her eyes widened. 'You're going after the grandfather?'

He eyed her. 'Contrary to what you may think, I don't go around annihilating every opponent who crosses my path, Elise.'

She flushed. 'I'll see what I can do.'

'You'll do better than that. You insist on reminding me of the terms of your contract, so let *me* remind *you* that your contract holds as long as you remain useful to me. Find me something I can use, or you'll cease to be useful.'

The warning gripped the back of her mind all morning and afternoon, long after the video conference that proved to be a colossal waste of time.

Ten minutes into the call, it was clear the Ishikawa brothers were merely spouting platitudes in order to buy themselves more time. She was surprised Alejandro went along with it, giving them the further week they requested to iron out what were clearly nonsensical minor issues.

Then he and the team spent the rest of the week digging deeper into every aspect of the Ishikawa Corporation.

Elise felt a moment's unease when the words *hostile takeover* were thrown on the table. Alejandro's head lifted and he stared directly at her as he vetoed the idea. She wasn't sure why her heart tripped over. Nothing had changed between them. Their Tuesday morning conversation had set a precedent for their stilted relationship.

Each morning, Alejandro gave her a different

brief. She clocked off late in the evening by presenting him with a carefully typed-out report.

He never invited her to dine with him in his private dining room. He never offered her a lift home.

She told herself she was glad about that. Very glad.

CHAPTER SIX

ALEJANDRO READ THE message on his phone for the fifth time as he stood before his window on Monday morning. For the umpteenth time, he wondered if he'd been right in contacting Gael in the first place. What had seemed like a sound idea—calling his brother to warn him he didn't intend to lose— in the early hours of Sunday morning coated his mouth with distaste a few short hours later.

He hadn't expected Gael's quick response, nor had he expected the request contained within his brother's email.

Gael wanted a meeting.

The stark request sounded more like an order. Clearly, his estranged brother hadn't lost his renowned arrogant swagger. As for the caveat that the meeting take no longer than fifteen minutes...

Pursing his lips, he dialled the number attached to the email. It was just after 6:30 a.m. on the east coast, which meant the middle of the night in California. With an unhealthy amount of relish, he pressed the phone to his ear.

It was answered on the fourth ring. 'Aguilar.'

His name on another's lips threatened an influx of memories. Memories that revolved around why his brother existed in the first place. Ruthlessly, he pushed them back.

'If I've disturbed your beauty sleep, just say the word and I'll call back at a more appropriate time,' he said.

He received a scoffing grunt in return. 'The only thing you've interrupted is a hearty breakfast, followed by a proper greeting of the woman currently warming my bed, both of which I intend to get back to in less than sixty seconds since I don't anticipate this call lasting any longer.'

'You make a habit of eating breakfast in the middle of the night?'

'The great thing about not having to answer to anyone is that I can do whatever the hell I want, when I want. But as it so happens, we're in the same time zone, *mi hermano*, so your concern about my digestive system is touching, but unwarranted.'

Alejandro gritted his teeth at the familial term, wondering why Gael insisted on taunting him with a past he was sure they both wanted to forget. He'd never bothered to confirm the rumours behind Gael also leaving his childhood home in Spain the moment he'd reached adulthood, but they'd involved their father.

And yet, Gael never missed the chance to remind him they were related.

Dismissing the baited response, he carried on. 'About this meeting tomorrow—'

'I'll stretch it to half an hour if you wish. But no longer than that. I have back-to-back meetings in New York in the afternoon that I need to fly straight back for.'

Alejandro's mouth twisted. 'A face-to-face meeting needn't take place at all if you see reason and back off. Now.'

Terse silence greeted him. He knew the line hadn't dropped because he could hear Gael's steady breathing.

'Need I remind you that *you* contacted *me*?' his brother eventually snapped, a throb of annoyance in his voice.

Alejandro started to shrug, then stopped at the futile action. Unbidden, Elise's voice sliced across his mind.

The looking-into-the-whites-of-their-eyes approach...

It annoyed him greatly that snippets of their conversation darted into his thoughts when he least expected it. Even greater was the despised thought that perhaps one of those snippets was what had fed his desire to contact Gael. A decision he regretted with each passing second. 'I was mistaken to think you would pay better attention if we were face to face. But that would be disrespecting you. You can hear me just as succinctly over the phone. This has gone on for long enough.'

'And it will keep going until I win the merger. I'll be at your offices tomorrow as scheduled. I advise you to be there.'

'You'll do well not to issue threats, Gael.'

'Or what? You'll up sticks and relocate again?' There was a gruff note in his brother's voice that made Alejandro's brow twinge in a brief frown.

'I have no intention of going anywhere. What I'll do is pull out all the stops to end this if you don't back off.'

Gael laughed. 'I look forward to hearing all about it when I arrive in Chicago tomorrow. And don't bother sending your jet for me. I have one of my own.'

Alejandro braced one hand on the window, welcoming the cold glass's fractional calming of his turbulent emotions. Slowly he breathed out. 'Gael, I don't wish to go to war with you.'

Another pulse of silence ensued. 'This only ends

one way, brother. With one of us walking away. And I don't intend it to be me.'

Alejandro closed his eyes against the morning sun's glare. Behind him he heard the door open. He didn't need to turn around to know Elise had arrived, at precisely 6:45, as she'd done all last week. He also knew that he'd spend the day with his senses attuned to her every movement in her office, although his interactions with her would be clinically brief because those charged ten minutes last Tuesday morning had deeply unsettled him. To the point where he had still remained perplexed at his own behaviour hours later. To the point where he'd questioned his own sanity.

He'd almost kissed her.

Had almost dared her to kiss him in payment for obtaining her services. Even more deplorable, for those insane minutes, he hadn't cared about the potential damage he risked with his actions. Hadn't cared about the 'once bitten, twice shy' warning that had been the dogma of his professional relationships for a decade.

The need to taste her had been unrelenting. Consuming. He remained disconcerted that just beneath the surface of his interactions with her, the need still fiercely burned.

'Do you wish me to repeat that in Spanish,

hermano?' Gael's voice brought him back to earth. To the room. To the click of heels drawing closer.

'*Muy bien*, if this is the route you wish to take, then so be it.'

He ended the call and turned around.

Elise eyed him from her position before his desk. 'Good morning.'

He nodded tersely, then made a concerted effort to shake off the barrage of unwanted sensations evoked by his brother and Elise. '*Buenos días*. I trust you had a good weekend?'

Her eyes widened, no doubt because his cordial tone was unexpected. 'It was okay, nothing life-changing.'

'How unfortunate. Weekends that aren't life-changing ought to be stripped of their title and re-named Pointless Days.'

Her head tilted to one side. 'Is that your attempt at a joke, Alejandro?'

'Since you're not laughing, I must respond firmly in the negative,' he replied, his tone bone-dry.

Her mouth twitched, then she smiled. It was transformative enough to deliver a punch to his solar plexus, causing his breath to snag and the hairs on his arms to rise in near alarm.

Alejandro had dated women who could command the covers of fashion magazines with a snap of their fingers. And yet he was certain none of them could hold a candle to Elise's smile.

All the same, he shouldn't be this enthralled.

And yet...

'Are you okay?'

'Of course. Why should I not be?' he quipped.

Her smile dimmed. 'No reason. I just...overheard a little of your conversation. Something about not wishing to go to war?'

Any trace of mirth disappeared. 'Eavesdropping, Elise?'

'Not intentionally.' She glanced at his phone. 'Was that your brother?'

Her lack of fear when it came to him should've aggravated him. Sure, he tolerated the underlings who challenged him, but it was what he paid them to do.

Elise challenged him because she couldn't help herself. When she wasn't irritating him, Alejandro had found himself almost...refreshed by her.

But not right now.

'Yes,' he replied, paradoxically going against his better judgment of telling himself he owed her no answers.

A soft look entered her eyes. 'And?'

His mouth twisted. 'As predicted, he refuses to listen to reason.'

'So he's just like you, then?'

Alejandro stiffened. 'Excuse me?'

She shrugged. 'You're both determined to win.'

'You say that as if there's something wrong with winning.'

'What's wrong is you gripping that phone as if you're about to crush it. You want to win, yes, but I'm guessing not if it's costing you this much.'

He glanced down and visibly unclenched his fingers from the handset. 'You guess wrong. Pain and the cost of winning only affect you if you give them the power to,' he replied, then froze at the words that had left his lips without permission.

Elise's eyes rounded. 'Unless there's a mind trick you picked up along the way to dull it, no one is immune from pain.'

A note in her voice tweaked his flaring senses. 'When have you known pain?' he asked, then realised he was holding his breath for her answer.

Her gaze flicked away from him. 'I'm human. I feel pain.'

The thought that she'd been hurt shouldn't have abraded his equilibrium. And yet it did.

'You seek specifics from me, yet generalise about yourself.'

'I was just pointing out you're not the only one with issues, professionally or personally.' She jerked towards the drinks trolley and picked up a bottle of water.

Alejandro frowned. 'You have a professional issue with me?'

She looked up from toying with the lid. 'What? No. I mean…I like to think our differences have been aired successfully.'

The slow drag in his groin as his gaze landed on her lips informed him his success in that department was distinctly lacking.

'Then what do you mean?'

Nerves clearly fuelled her sudden twitchiness. 'I don't want to talk about it.'

An answer that birthed further burning questions. 'Did something happen to you?'

Her cheeks lost a little colour, but her face closed mutinously. 'Nothing I want to reprise. What's on the agenda today?' she hurriedly asked.

It took a huge dose of the willpower he was renowned for to step back from demanding answers from her. Even then, he needed a minute before he tracked properly.

'Since we're biding our time till our next call with the Ishikawa brothers, I'd like your help on another matter. Are you free this evening to accompany me to a client dinner?'

She blinked. 'Uh…yes.'

'Good. Reservations are for seven. Feel free to leave early today if you need to. I'll pick you up from your apartment just before seven.'

'Okay. Will the purpose of the dinner be damage limitation or image enhancement?'

'A little bit of both. I'm meeting a client and his wife for dinner. She's taken to overt displays of affection whenever I'm in her company. He's chosen to encourage it in the hope that I'll do business with him. My patience is wearing thin but I'd like to put a stop to both without jeopardising our business relationship. You think you can handle that?'

Her relief at the changed subject turned to shock, but she rallied after a few seconds. 'Sure. Of course.'

Alejandro nodded briskly, despite his continued mental state of flux. He needed to emulate her, and regroup quickly. Gael's imminent arrival should be what commanded his entire focus, not the banked anguish still shadowing Elise's eyes.

Heading for his desk, he provided her with the client names and watched her walk away. The suit she wore today was feminine and stylish. Beneath the edge of her jacket, the trousers cradled her pert backside and emphasised her curvy hips. When she shed the jacket upon reaching her desk, he caught a glimpse of her trim waist and the full swell of her breasts.

A sound, rough and unwelcome, punched up from his throat.

She started to look his way.

He dragged his gaze away and focused on the pile of work on his desk. She was off limits. And even outside the scope of their professional relationship were he to consider her for an affair, he would still reject the idea.

Because Elise Jameson exhibited signs he'd hitherto not encountered in a woman before—she had the potential to get under his skin.

He reminded himself of that fact as his chauffeured limo pulled up to her apartment building that evening, an irritably large proportion of him anticipating her presence.

Her smile…

He shook himself free of the low sizzle in his stomach and stepped out. Seeing the unlatched main doors, a different type of irritation surged. He pressed her buzzer none too gently.

'I'll be right down.'

Since he wasn't sure whether the lift functioned with any efficiency tonight, he kept his attention between it and the stairs, flatly refusing to acknowledge the rising thrum in his blood.

Heels on the stairs alerted him to her mode of

descent. She arrived at the top of the last flight of stairs and his heart rate increased.

She wasn't smiling.

In fact she appeared distinctly nervous.

Yet, she was captivatingly breathtaking.

Her chocolate-brown hair was swept to one side of her face and pinned at the back in a loose style that left several tresses falling free to caress her neck. Her knee-length dress, made of dark green material, skimmed her hips but hugged her breasts and left her shoulders bare. A simple necklace drew attention to her slim neck. In one hand she held a wrap and purse, her other hand clinging to the rail as she came down. He wasn't aware he'd moved until she paused on the stairs. Her gaze met his as she slid her hand into the one he held out.

'Thank you,' she murmured.

'*De nada*. Breaking your neck before the first course is served would be extremely bad form.'

A hint of a smile appeared. 'Wow. Two jokes in one day. Do we need to notify record keepers in some obscure office?'

He found his mouth curving. 'Best not. We wouldn't want to incite any unnatural disasters.'

A full-blown smile appeared. Something vibrated in the region of his chest. Keeping her hand in his, he led her to his car, choosing not to mention the state of her lobby security. Or lack thereof.

And if a part of him suddenly wished their dinner involved two less people, he brushed it away under the guise of it being a temporary aberration.

They arrived at Millennia, one of Chicago's most lauded restaurants, ahead of Jeff and Mindy Stoneley, for which Elise was just a tiny bit grateful. It gave her a chance to gather herself. To deliver a much-needed pep talk that involved *not* getting carried away with what was happening tonight.

This *wasn't* a date.

It was *business*.

She was doing work for which she was being *paid*.

PR work held many facets. Fact. When she was a newly employed member of Jameson, her parents had inundated her at all hours with absurd requests before she'd finally put her foot down.

'You're frowning. Is the venue not to your liking?'

'What? Oh, no. It's not that. This is great!' She noted the gushiness in her voice and dialled it down. 'I'm sure your clients will appreciate it.'

Alejandro's narrow-eyed speculation didn't abate. 'But something disturbed you just then.'

She tried to wave it away. 'I was just remembering some of the things I had to do when I started working at Jameson.'

'Are you referring to the incident you didn't wish to speak of before?' he asked, still narrow-eyed.

Her heart missed a beat, the thought that she'd nearly spilled her guts to Alejandro earlier today stabbing discomfort through her. Determinedly, she pushed it away. 'No. I meant something else,' she murmured, fervently hoping he'd let the matter drop.

'Something that doesn't compare favourably to this?'

'Are you kidding? Dining in a Michelin-starred restaurant beats getting up at two a.m. to go rescue a client's dog from the airport because our paparazzi-fleeing client had left it behind.'

He frowned. 'You're serious.'

'As frostbite.'

'Isn't that more of a minder's job?'

She shrugged. 'It is. I found out later.'

'How?' he asked.

Her mood dimmed further at the recollection. 'My parents were trying to teach me a lesson.'

'A lesson? Or punishment?' He cut through the excuse.

'Does it matter?'

'*Sí*. It does. And I'm guessing this wasn't a one-off event?'

She shook her head.

'Why did they do that?'

'They found out that I had graduated with two degrees, not one.'

'Surely that's a cause for celebration?'

Her heart lurched. 'You'd think so, wouldn't you?' she muttered. Realising they'd arrived at another subject she didn't relish probing too deeply, she cleared her throat, intending to steer him away from the testy issue of her parents, but Alejandro beat her to the punch.

'You only list one degree on your résumé.'

'Because it's the only one that's relevant to my present job.'

'Or it's the one that invites the least scrutiny?'

Her gaze rose from where she'd feigned interest in the place setting and met shrewd green eyes. 'You're digging, Alejandro. I may be tempted to dig back.'

'Will you be divulging anything that isn't already public knowledge?'

'No…but that's not what I meant.'

One shoulder lifted. 'You can tell me or I can unearth the truth myself.'

'Okay, it was an art degree.' Elise wasn't sure

why admitting that stirred a deeply buried hurt. Probably because a once-precious dream had been desiccated while she'd been scrambling to be done with her current reality.

'Impressive. And do you use it—'

'There you are. Apologies for being late, *bello*! Please say you'll forgive me? The car service was atrocious. I'm never using that firm again. Oh...I didn't realise this would be a *foursome*.'

Alejandro rose, albeit with minimal enthusiasm, as Mindy Stoneley paused dramatically at the table, her wide grey eyes assessing Elise.

Behind her, her husband, a giant of a man with thinning hair and a face that leant towards excess, cracked out a forced laugh.

'Careful, Mindy. You might give the impression we live a risqué lifestyle.'

Mindy ignored him and held out both hands to Alejandro. When he bent towards her, she pressed her lips to his.

The sharp dart of disquiet that went through Elise held her in place for several paralysing heartbeats, only easing when Alejandro stepped back from Mindy's embrace.

'Jeff, Mindy, allow me to introduce you to Elise Jameson.'

Mindy sniffed, the skintight sequinned dress that

stopped a good foot above her knees rising even further as she leaned over and offered her hand to Elise. 'And what exactly is your connection to *Alejandro*?'

Elise cringed at the forced eroticism of Alejandro's name. 'I'm afraid that's confidential. But I hope you don't mind me joining you tonight. I've been dying to try the food here and Alejandro kindly offered to bring me along.'

'The offer wasn't generated by kindness, *querida*,' Alejandro drawled, his gaze lingering suggestively on her as he sat back down.

Her pulse leapt wildly, despite the clear evidence that his words were only for show.

Mindy's gaze swung to Alejandro as she and Jeff took their seats across from them. 'Alejandro *is* generous like that, isn't he? He's personally opened so many doors for us. I don't know how on earth we'll ever be able to thank him.' Her hand found Alejandro's on the table, her 'gratitude' lingering a touch too long before Alejandro removed his own hand.

The knot in his jaw equalled that in Elise's throat. She looked up in relief as the head waiter approached.

The first course of Cajun fusion food arrived. Alejandro directed the conversation towards business as often as Mindy tried to direct it to the personal.

Jeff drank more and the atmosphere grew tense.

Cognisant of the extent of Alejandro's temper, Elise racked her brain for something to alleviate the tension. When Mindy invited Alejandro to come and inspect her newly built steam room for the third time, Elise shifted her seat closer and placed her hand on Alejandro's arm, his earlier statement lending her the bravery to risk the move.

Gleaming green eyes darted to her. Mindy stopped speaking. Jeff rushed in to fill the taut silence.

Elise leaned in, her mouth a whisper from his ear. 'I'm sorry. I'm doing my best to steer her away from you,' she murmured, 'but short of crawling into your lap and performing a lewd act on you, this is the only way I can think of to get her to back off. Do me a favour and pretend you're enjoying the sweet nothings I'm whispering in your ear?'

He didn't move. Or respond. Horror dredged through her, colour surging up her cheeks as seconds stretched.

Beneath her hold, his muscles flexed. Then he turned and aligned his face with hers. His breath washed over her neck as his neat stubble brushed her cheek. Strong fingers found hers on his arm, strangling her breath as he murmured, 'Crawling into my lap isn't the worst idea I've heard, but perhaps the timing isn't quite right for that. And these aren't sweet nothings. They're extremely useful *somethings* that could do the trick.'

Her breath caught. She started to move away. He held her still.

'No. Stay. And don't look now, *guapa*. You'll ruin the effect.' Slowly, his mouth drifted light kisses along her jaw to the corner of her mouth, then returned along the same trail to the pulse beating beneath her ear.

Elise, not having taken a breath in almost a minute, felt her heart hammering against her ribs as she held still and let him deliver his message. The drugging excitement that launched through her veins was a mere by-product of this act, she assured herself. Once Alejandro was done, sanity would be restored.

After an interminable age, where Mindy cleared her throat more than a few times, Alejandro finally pulled back.

'I didn't realise you two were a *thing*,' Mindy said after a brief moment of sullen silence.

Alejandro, his hand still locking hers into place, replied, 'We aren't just a *thing*, Mindy. We're exclusive.' He sent Elise a heat-filled glance.

The Stoneleys departed shortly after that. When Elise refused coffee, Alejandro requested the bill. Elise excused herself to visit the ladies' room and was returning when a shadow fell across her path.

'I see you're practising your moves on another chump.' The statement was delivered with a sinister laugh she'd hoped to never hear again. 'I'm surprised, though. I credited Aguilar with more sense.'

Ice filled her veins as her gaze snapped up to meet Brian Grey's. A part of her urged a swift retreat back into the ladies' room. Or a quick dive past the heavyset man back to the safety of the restaurant and Alejandro.

But she'd stood up to him once, had fought tooth and nail to prevent a life-altering assault. And though her insides shook alarmingly, Elise didn't back down.

'Your self-esteem must be at an all-time low if you're referring to yourself as a chump. Just proves money can't buy you everything, huh, Brian?'

Arctic-blue eyes that gleamed a little too brightly snapped pure hatred at her. 'I see you still haven't learnt your lesson. Maybe I should've put more effort into teaching it to you last year.'

Anger and pain fought for supremacy within her. Cold anger won. 'And I should've delivered *two* knee-to-groin responses instead of one?'

His face reddened. His shadow loomed larger as he reached for her.

Fighting panic, she stepped back. Into strong, solid arms.

'Everything okay, Elise?' Alejandro drawled.

Relief punched through her despite the latent danger she heard in his voice. Whirling, she looked up into his rigid face. 'Can we go now?'

He didn't answer. His gaze remained pinned on Brian, his eyes coldly assessing.

'Alejandro, please?'

His glance shifted to her. Elise knew her emotions were displayed clearly for him to see, but she just wanted to leave Brian's unpleasant presence.

After a beat, Alejandro nodded and settled his hand in the small of her back.

The walk through the restaurant and into the back of the limo was conducted in silence. As were the first ten minutes of the journey.

But tacit questions churned through the air. When he finally turned to her, her stomach dipped.

'Grey was the professional issue you spoke of.'

It was a question disguised as a statement. But she didn't want to answer. 'Please, can you let it be?'

'No.' He caught her chin between his fingers. 'Answer me, *por favor*.'

She grimaced at the politely couched command.

When she shook her head, his face hardened. 'You can tell me or we can return to the restaurant and I can ask him myself.'

'Alejandro…' She stopped at the intractable expression on his face.

'Now, Elise.'

She sucked in a steadying breath. 'You mentioned him by name so you know who he is and what he does?'

He nodded. 'He runs nightclubs but recently added a clothes line to his business, is that correct?'

She nodded. 'Mostly lingerie. He contracted Jameson to help launch his lingerie line last year.'

He released her chin, but his gaze didn't waver from her face. 'And?'

'My father and I worked on the campaign for the first month. Then Brian requested that I take over. I didn't think anything of it.'

Alejandro's jaw clenched. 'Go on.'

She stopped when she realised they'd pulled up in front of her building. Alejandro noticed, too, and made a rough sound of impatience.

'We'll continue this inside,' he snapped.

The walk to her apartment was rushed and silent. He requested her keys and unlocked her door. 'Invite me in,' he muttered, his low voice tight.

Tension gripped Elise, but, because she didn't

want to conduct the rest of the traumatic tale on her doorstep, she cleared her throat and stepped into her apartment. 'Come in.'

He followed, kicking the door shut.

Her one-bedroom apartment was compact, decorated with whatever money she could spare after rent and loan payments. The living room held a single faux-velvet sofa, matching armchair and floor rugs. The pale walls were brightened with cheap landscapes, and floor and table lamps softened the starkness of the battered cabinet on which perched her TV and MP3 player.

Alejandro didn't spare the room a single glance. His gaze remained fixed on her, tweaking her already frazzled nerves.

'Would you...umm...like a drink?'

'No.' He came forward, took her wrap and purse from her nerveless fingers. 'Sit down, Elise.'

He was ordering her around in her own home. Part of her wanted to stomp on his autocracy. A greater part wanted this over with.

She sat. He shrugged off his coat, draped it over the armchair, leaving on the bespoke dinner suit. She dragged her gaze from his intrinsically masculine form as he sat down next to her. 'Finish.'

A knot twisted inside her as unpleasant memories flooded her. 'He wanted to hold the launch at one of his nightclubs. I went there to take pictures for the press packets. He suggested I'd get a better sense of his style if I tried on some of his lingerie. I refused.'

She ventured a glance at Alejandro.

His face was a rigid mask of fury. 'And?'

'He...insisted.'

'How?' he rasped.

Elise shivered. 'He...restrained me. Said he wouldn't let me leave until I gave him what he wanted.'

Alejandro surged to his feet. *'Madre de Dios!'* He paced her living room in a tight circle, one hand slashing through his hair. Mid-pace, he jolted to a stop. 'Did he...?'

Elise shook her head. 'I... It didn't get that far.'

'Did you report him to the authorities?' he jerked out.

Pain lanced her. 'Yes. But he wasn't charged.'

Darkness clouded his eyes. 'Why the *hell* not?'

'He had cameras in his nightclub, but he knew how to position himself so his actions seemed benign. And the parts where I fought back were out of shot. Also...' She stopped.

'What?'

'He *encouraged* my parents it would be in Jameson's interest if they convinced me to drop the allegations.'

'*Your parents?* And did they?'

'They didn't have to. The case fell apart on its own.'

'*Dios mio,*' he breathed.

Elise had no idea tears had slipped free until he sat back down and cradled her face in his hands.

His thumbs dried her tears as he regarded her. 'You're strong and intelligent. You will *not* let this damage you,' he declared.

She sniffed. 'Aren't we all damaged in some way?'

A solemn look entered his eyes. '*Sí,* we are. But yours shouldn't centre on this. The bastard shouldn't even cross your thoughts, never mind reduce you to tears.'

She blinked rapidly, unwilling to show how his words affected her. 'I told you I didn't want to talk about it,' she murmured.

A hint of regret washed over his face. '*Lo siento,* but you intrigue me in many ways, Elise. I couldn't help myself.'

She didn't have a response for that because his expression was changing, morphing from anger into something equally powerful. Something that caused her breath to shorten, then hitch in her throat.

His hand slid to her nape.

'Elise.' Her name was a deep intonation that drew a shudder from her.

She met his fiery green gaze. Her mouth parted on a needy little whimper. His eyes latched on her lips and the air thickened with sensual promise.

He was going to kiss her. She wasn't going to stop him.

Because…because…

Reason dissolved into mist the moment his mouth seared hers. Firm, chiselled and lush. His kiss went from exploratory to demanding in a flash. He groaned when her head fell back and she let him in.

One hand captured her waist, pulled her in closer, until she was plastered against him.

The elevated beat of his heart echoed against her chest.

Elise squirmed as she drowned in the power and magic of Alejandro's kiss. She wriggled closer, moaning when his tongue stroked hers with an urgent expertise that arrowed pleasure straight between her thighs. Growing more desperate by the minute for an unattainable pleasure, she slipped her hands beneath his jacket. His warm cotton-covered flesh was hers to explore.

And explore she did, until the need for air forced them apart.

Alejandro stared down at her with drugged, fierce eyes. '*Dios*, you taste incredible.'

Another blush, hotter and faster, surged into her cheeks.

He laughed low and deep, passing his thumbs over her cheeks. 'And you blush like an innocent. A seriously lethal innocent.'

Before she could respond, he was kissing her again, bearing her back on the seat. She gave herself over, happily swapping unwanted memories in favour of *this*. Kissing Alejandro brought no pain. Touching him filled her with excitement. Joy.

Her hands slid up to his broad shoulders. His hair. Spiking her fingers through it, she let out a little cry as his hand cupped her breast. Somewhere along the line, her dress had shifted, her strapless bra exposed to his clever fingers. Alejandro's mouth left hers, and she stared, dazed and engrossed, as he slowly moved back one lace cup to expose a budded pink nipple.

Her breath strangled as he caught the peak between his fingers. Need arrowed straight to the apex of her thighs. Then he lowered his head and, eyes riveted on hers, took her nipple in his mouth.

Sensation exploded through her, arching her in a tight bow, and feeding him more of herself.

Alejandro uttered a pained groan as he suckled

her. One hand slid beneath her to hold her to his rapt attention, while the other wandered feverishly down her body. His fingers trailed fire over her bare thighs as his mouth drifted across the slope of one breast to capture the peak of the other.

Desire throbbed at her core, drowning her in rabid need.

From one frantic heartbeat to the next, his fingers slipped beneath her panties to graze her damp flesh.

Elise cried out, a fever like she'd never known flooding her.

'*Dios mio, bella dama*, you intoxicate me.'

One finger breached her core. Elise tensed, a different sensation racing down her spine. She wanted to block it out, but the flashing sign in her brain wouldn't let her.

...you blush like an innocent...

Except she wasn't *like* one. Her virginity was something she'd guarded with almost zealous care before the incident with Brian. Not because she was hung up on giving it to the right man, but because it was the one thing, besides her art, that affirmed to her that she was nothing like her parents. After Brian, she was even more wary about her sexuality. She would never succumb to casual pleasures.

Not even with the most charismatic man she'd ever met.

She pushed at his shoulders. 'No. Stop!' When he stared at her with a puzzled frown, she shook her head. 'I can't do this.'

His eyes slowly cleared. When his fingers left her core and he sat back in the seat, Elise bit her lip to stop from protesting.

'*Sí*, I know. I'm breaking my own rules.'

He believed she'd called a halt because of her contract with SNV.

Elise shakily exhaled. 'You misunderstand. I wouldn't sleep with you even without your rules. This shouldn't have happened. And it won't happen again…ever.'

Every last trace of lust left his face and with each passing second, a greater part of her mourned. He stood, shoved his hands deep in his pockets and stared down at her as she scrambled up and righted her clothes.

'Explain.'

'Do I need to? You caught me at a low moment—'

Tension clamped his frame. '*Perdón?* Are you suggesting I took advantage of you?' His voice was clipped with ice. 'If so, let me remind you that you were with me every step of the way, *guapa*.'

A hint of shame slammed her. 'I think it's time we brought the evening to an end. I've gone above and beyond my duties for one day, I believe.'

'If this is a taster of what your *duties* could be, perhaps we should renegotiate your contract. I'm sure we can agree to a mutually benefitting addendum.'

She gasped, ice dredging through her insides. 'You didn't just say that to me.'

His eyes gleamed, an unfathomable emotion flickering in his eyes. 'We're laying our cards on the table. I want you. I believe the feeling is mutual. We can wait until the merger is over. Or we can agree to terms now.'

'I don't want to agree to any further terms with you. And I'm sorry if your ego doesn't like hearing no from a nobody like me.'

Impossibly, he stiffened further. 'You wouldn't be making the mistake of likening me to that bastard, would you, Elise?' he murmured with deathly calm.

The smooth lethality of it froze her vocal cords for a few seconds too long. His face lost a shade of colour and his jaw clenched tight.

'Alejandro, I'm—'

'Save your breath. You can deny it all you want, but you took as much as you gave tonight. And you knew the precise moment to call a halt to achieve maximum effect.' His mouth twisted in a cruel smile. 'That skill has to come from somewhere, right?'

She hadn't thought hearing the words she'd dreaded most and had heard whispered about her would hurt coming from Alejandro. But it stung deeper than it ever had.

She rose, willing her legs not to give way, and walked to the door. Turning the handle, she threw it open. 'And here I thought you were enlightened enough to realise that sometimes the apple *does* fall far from the tree. How disappointing. I'm glad I could be of extra-curricular service to you tonight. Do me a favour and let's keep things strictly business from now on, shall we?'

He didn't deign to utter a response. Cold eyes raked her from head to toe. Then he strode out with arrogant indifference.

Elise slammed the door hard. And even before she turned the key, she was cursing the hot scald of tears choking her.

CHAPTER SEVEN

ELISE SLEPT THROUGH her alarm and woke up at seven-thirty. The ominous start to the day thankfully didn't earn her Alejandro's scorn because he wasn't in the office when she hurried in just after quarter past eight. She breathed a sigh of relief when Margo informed her he would be out of the office all morning.

She got on with putting finishing touches to the work she'd left unfinished yesterday. As she recalled the unfortunate end to the evening, her heart dipped with disappointment and hurt.

Enough! Knowing she would always be in some way tarred with the same brush when it came to her parents, she'd learned to toughen up at an early age. Alejandro had merely lucked out and cornered her in a weak moment after coercing her to spill her guts about Brian.

Nothing more.

When the words continued to echo hollowly at the back of her mind, Elise decided to use her free time for the head-clearing run she hadn't managed that morning. She struck out for nearby Millennium Park, the exertion and the light April breeze doing an effective job of clearing her tension and lending a little perspective.

Last night, she'd got carried away. She'd glimpsed sympathy that had been sorely lacking on all fronts following Brian's assault and had grasped it with both hands. Then she'd followed it by falling into a web of sexual attraction while ignoring the accompanying pitfalls.

But she had put on the brakes. There was nothing to feel guilty about. If anything, Alejandro's attitude was what should be causing her grief. And yet, all through the night of tossing and turning, that fleeting expression on his face had haunted her. Continued to haunt her. For a single moment, just before he'd accused her of comparing him to Brian, she'd glimpsed a sharp pain, felt an alignment of her own hurt. As much as she wanted to dismiss it, the notion wouldn't die. Nor could she deny his sympathy and comfort had been genuine.

But afterwards…

Was she attributing more humanity to him than was warranted? Accepting her thoughts were going around in futile circles, she completed her run, performed her stretches, and returned to SNV.

She walked through the doors and was crossing

the foyer to the drink fountain when she saw Alejandro.

Except it wasn't Alejandro.

The hair, stature and innate confidence that were imprinted on him were almost identical. But apart from the visual confirmation when the man turned from calling for the lift, her stomach didn't quite dive and clench the same way it did in Alejandro's presence.

This was Alejandro's brother. The resemblance was uncanny. All the way down to his lifted eyebrow when he realised he was the object of scrutiny.

Her very blatant scrutiny.

A very male, very confident smile curved his lips as he abandoned the lift and sauntered towards her. His return scrutiny didn't make her skin prickle the way Alejandro's did, but nevertheless Elise grew conscious of the cling of Lycra and sheen of sweat coating her skin.

'A beautiful woman who shows dedication in taking care of herself is a sexy thing to behold.'

His voice, so much like Alejandro's, but also so different, made her smile emerge a little weaker than usual. 'You don't know me from a lamp post, so what makes you think I'm in any way dedicated? For all you know this could be the start of a very late New Year's resolution.'

His gaze drifted from her head to the tips of her trainers and back again. 'Then I commend you for the excellent, decidedly non-lamp-post-like framework you're building on.' His words held the same Spanish intonation that curled around Alejandro's.

Laughter bubbled up, easy and unexpected, providing a touch of relief from her roiling thoughts. 'I'm not sure whether to thank you for the compliment or roll my eyes at that smooth line.'

'Gael Aguilar.' He held out his hand. 'And you wound me.'

She shook his hand. 'You're Alejandro's brother,' she confirmed.

A shadow crossed Gael's features. 'For my sins, yes.'

A sixth sense warned her his words were meant literally. The lift arrived and she stepped into the small space beside him. She couldn't help but notice with every floor that passed, his tension escalated.

This brother wasn't anticipating an amicable meeting.

And with Alejandro, was there any other kind?

Elise cleared her throat. 'I hope you can sort things out with the Japanese deal.'

His eyes hardened for a moment, before he smiled. 'That outcome would depend entirely on my brother.'

She frowned.

'You look shocked. What has my brother been telling you about me?'

'Nothing, save that he expects the same thing from you.'

A smile, icy but tinged with a hint of bleakness, tweaked his lips. 'What can I say? We're not known for giving quarter,' he rasped.

The doors opened and they stepped into the hallway. 'It was—'

'Elise!'

They both turned at the thunderous summons. Heat and ice invaded her body, both bringing equally painful awareness, as Alejandro's incandescent gaze slashed over her, dashed to his brother, and then remained fixed on Gael.

Alejandro had never experienced possessiveness about anyone or anything in his life. Sure, he was attached to the success he'd worked hard for, but he possessed nothing in life that would cause him physical pain to part with. He'd learned at a very early age that affection or material things given one day could be taken away the next with no rhyme or reason. Every occurrence in his life as a child had revolved around whether his mother had decided to be happy, or whether she was locked into playing the wronged wife, visiting her misery and pain on everyone around her. And that had solely depended on whether his father was in the mood to reprise his role of philanderer or not.

Everything in his life had been coated with a transience that had forced him to create a bubble around himself. Because if he get didn't attached in the first place, he wouldn't feel the loss. The logic was absurdly simple.

But for some reason, right from the very beginning, he'd detested the interest Elise garnered from every single person she came into contact with. Acknowledging the curious problem privately to himself hadn't seen it diminish. Getting a taste of her last night and then being forced to walk away, after realising just how transient *she* was, had done something to him. He couldn't place his finger on what it was, save for the knowledge that she'd stirred something so powerful and turbulent within him, he hadn't been able to concentrate worth a damn all day.

Seeing her standing next to his brother, Gael's barely disguised interest in her visible even across the space between them, Alejandro wanted to breach the distance, claim her by branding his name on the skin she didn't have any qualms about exposing, in the most blatant way possible. That bubble of self-denial he'd existed in was gone, leaving a stone labelled *Need* in his gut, which seemed to grow heavier with each second.

Dios. This was beyond unacceptable.

'Did you want something, Alejandro?' Elise said, her chin lifted in challenge.

'Other than to request that you be at your desk where you're *supposed* to be?'

Her eyes darkened, her gaze flickering to Gael with a touch of embarrassment. A second later, her lips pursed. 'Sorry, my bad. I thought the shackles attached to my desk were for decorative purposes only. Let me change out of my running gear and I'll get back on the workhorse.'

He caught Gael's low chuckle, but he couldn't look at his brother. Not when the sight of Elise approaching ripped his senses wide open with voracious hunger, reminding him of her scent, her responsiveness beneath his touch.

He dragged his gaze from her hips, forced his scrutiny up past her luscious breasts, her slender neck, to her face, and locked his knees to remain upright.

Every day since her first day at SNV, she'd arrived fully but impeccably made-up. Today, her face held the barest hint of artificial colour. Her skin glowed with a natural beauty, her eyes even more vivid without the added frills.

Gael had seen her like this first...

Irrational, primitive jealousy threatened to shame him, but it was shoved aside by other emotions rippling through him.

Emotions that involved his brother.

His eyes finally shifted to Gael. Lingered against his will. A tug pulled at him deep inside. In the decade since they'd last seen each other, his brother had grown in resemblance to the man Alejandro himself saw every day when he looked in the mirror.

A carbon copy of their father. The man who'd betrayed his family over and over again.

He admitted to himself that the resemblance made it hard for him to look at Gael. Alejandro also admitted it might have contributed to him leaving California all those years ago. Acceptance of that flaw made him swallow. And wish he'd never sent that email suggesting a meeting.

'I'm here, Andro,' Gael stated when they were six feet from each other. 'Are we going to waste the day imitating a Mexican standoff or are you going to make me an offer I can't refuse?'

Alejandro thrust his clenched fists into his pockets, willing his gaze not to stray to Elise as she walked past and headed for the changing room. When the door swung shut behind her, he narrowed his eyes at his brother. 'We'll take the meeting in my office. And don't call me that.'

Gael's lips pursed as he fell into step beside him. 'Still as touchy as ever, I see. It's surprising you've managed to pull off a few impressive deals over the years while wearing your emotions on your sleeve.'

Alejandro slammed his office door and faced Gael. 'What the hell are you talking about?' he snapped.

'It's obvious you have a thing for that gorgeous creature out there, and don't bother denying it. For a second there, you looked ready to drop kick me. I'm guessing the rumours about you being a shark in the boardroom are false, then?' Gael taunted.

Alejandro forced his shoulders to relax. Going to the drinks cabinet, he poured two shots of single malt whisky and held one out to Gael. His brother accepted his with one raised eyebrow, but didn't drink it.

Alejandro downed his in one go, memories of last night almost pushing him into slamming the glass down. 'There's nothing going on between Elise and I. She's here to do a specific job. Once her usefulness is expended, she'll be duly compensated and disposed of. End of story.'

Gael gave a low whistle as he strolled confidently to the window. 'Consider my concerns about your softness revised.' He appreciated the view for a long minute, then turned. 'I don't intend to back down on the Japanese deal. Toredo needs this deal—'

'Your company specialises in offering streaming media and cloud-based services. It's not an e-commerce outfit like mine *or* Ishikawa Corp. There are a dozen companies you can merge with that better suit your business—'

'But none with a similar foothold in Asia,' Gael countered. 'This has the potential to be the perfect merger for me to combine e-commerce with streaming media.' He shrugged. 'I'm yet to be convinced there's a downside to it.'

Alejandro pursed his lips. 'I'll repeat what I said to you yesterday.' The bite of further frustration made him slash a hand through his hair, uncaring whether the sign made him appear anything other than in total control. 'There will be other deals. I'll help you secure the next one, if you need it. Walk away from this one.'

Gael's lips curled and his fingers tightened around the glass. 'I haven't asked for or needed your aid for a long time, not since I came to you for help in finding my mother when I was thirteen and you turned me down flat.'

Another tug in his chest, this time one he recognised as guilt, made him tense, even while his frustration grew. 'You accuse me of being soft, and yet you can't seem to let go of the past. I didn't want to get involved in your mess then, and I want to even less now.'

Gael's jaw clenched. 'You knew where she was, Andro. Despite our father lying through his teeth that he wasn't with her, you knew they were shacked up in that godforsaken apartment he kept on the side for his mistresses. For three weeks, I had to live with not knowing whether she was alive or dead.'

Alejandro's face stiffened, his whole body numb as he held himself rigidly in the present. 'You found her in the end, did you not?' he bit out.

'No thanks to you. You made it clear then that I was nothing to you. That you didn't even want the whiff of this bastard brother anywhere near you. I got the message loud and clear.'

Alejandro gritted his teeth. 'Regardless of what your imagination conjured up, I had my hands full with other matters.' Like keeping his mother from going off the deep end when she realised once again that her husband's promises of fidelity meant nothing.

Gael's mouth twisted as he set the glass down without drinking the whisky. '*Sí*, ensuring your popularity as the school's soccer star was firmly in place so you could continue dating the hottest girls was much more important than helping me out when I needed it. If your best offer is to tell me to walk away, then this meeting has been a colossal waste of my time.' He flicked a glance at his watch. 'I guess I'll be on my way. Thanks for the drink.'

Quick strides saw him at the door before Alejandro exhaled. 'What will it take?'

Gael froze. *'Que?'*

'For you to drop this deal. What will it take?'

His brother's hazel eyes turned a dark, dangerous green. 'We're blood, Andro. There's no bribe on earth that will remove that fact. And no amount of money that will appease my need to see you lose. Just once. *Hasta luego,*' he threw in sarcastically, before the door slammed behind him.

Alejandro braced his hands on top of the desk, his chest expanding and contracting for a full minute, before he dropped into his chair.

He'd expected it to go better. And of all the reminders of Gael he'd wanted to avoid, the reference to those hellish weeks was at the top of his list. Because that was the time when he'd finally accepted his father was beyond redemption. That his mother cared more about steeping herself in the frenzied, dysfunctional state of her marriage than she did about her son.

Bitterness, awakened and rancid, dredged through him. His fist curled on top of the file on his desk as he fought it back down. He wasn't sure how long he stayed that way, his gaze turned inward in memory.

The sound of the door opening and shutting, followed by the click of heels, finally dragged him from his unwanted musings.

She'd changed into a dress. Some sort of grey wool blend, high-necked thing that ended just above her knee and left her slender arms exposed. On her wrist a delicate bracelet drew his attention to her soft skin. He'd touched that skin last night. Tasted it.

Still hungered for it.

Reining in his unwanted craving, he watched her cross to her office. Alejandro found himself upright and following her before he'd fully computed the move. She was leaning over her desk, stretching for a file when he reached the doorway. Leaning against the frame, he questioned for the umpteenth time what it was about her that drove this unchecked compulsion within him.

She turned, and jumped. 'Uh...I didn't see you there.' She thrust the file she held at him. 'This is what I was working on this morning. I wouldn't like you to think I was idling away the time while you were out of the office.'

He took the file. 'I owe you an apology. Last night…I shouldn't have reacted quite so—'

'Ogre-tastically?'

Despite himself, a smile attempted to lift his mood. 'I was going to say "unprofessionally". My apologies.'

Her strikingly long lashes swept down for a moment. 'And I would've been better advised to keep things from getting too…personal.'

The reminder that there was something he needed to do had him striding forward to her desk to press the intercom.

'Sir?'

'Draft a memo to the marketing department. I want all contracts with Brian Grey's company terminated immediately.'

Elise gasped.

'Umm…yes, sir.'

He hung up. She stared at him, her parted lips trembling for a second before her gaze dropped. 'I don't need you to fight my battles for me, Alejandro.'

'And yet, it is done,' he stated, the rage that burned in his gut threatening to erupt all over again. His emotions when he'd left Elise last night had skittered close to the edge. Returning to the restaurant to confront the bastard had been high on his list but he accepted that satisfaction from violence would be fleeting. But *this*…this was a good start. And he intended to pay the piece of scum back in many varied ways. As for what she'd said about her parents… His gut clenched harder. Parents were a subject he wasn't yet willing to touch.

Her stunning eyes rose to his once more. 'I… don't know what to say.'

'Then let's move on.'

She nodded after a moment. 'How did things go with your brother?'

His laugh was a touch self-deprecating. 'As badly as I suspected they would.'

She smoothed back her fringe, a nervous tic of hers he'd noticed. 'I'm guessing from that tight-jawed look you're wearing that you couldn't find any middle ground?'

'You sound disappointed, *guapa*. Perhaps you expect too much for a first meeting in ten years.'

Her eyes widened. 'That's how long it's been since you saw each other?'

Alejandro felt that twinge again. 'Yes.'

'Why?'

'He reminded me of a past I wanted to leave behind.'

'*Reminded?* As in the past tense?'

He frowned, caught off guard by the slip. Shaking his head, he changed the subject. 'Did you find me anything I can use?'

A look, almost of disappointment, crossed her face. 'Nothing that would aid your war, but there's something else. Before you use it though, can I just suggest that SNV and Toredo could be different arms of the same company? Is a three-way merger out of the question?'

'It's low on my list of ideal outcomes.'

Her gaze dropped, her smile as tight as her nod.

He traced her face for a minute, noting that, apart from lip gloss, she hadn't applied any more make-up when she'd changed. He curbed the urge to trace his fingers over her skin as he had last night.

She'd made her feelings more than clear. She wasn't interested in blurring the professional lines of their relationship. And he needed to relocate his little black book.

Opening the file, he speed-read through the half-dozen pages and paused when he reached the most interesting morsel of information. 'Grandma to the rescue again?'

A light blush washed her cheeks. 'I didn't see the harm in tapping a useful source.'

He closed the file. 'I'll take it under advisement. The conference call with the Ishikawas is in fifteen minutes. I want you there.' Not that he held out much hope that it'd be any more progressive than the last one.

Gael had drawn battle lines and he would be going all out to sink his claws deeper into the deal.

As expected, Alejandro was met with platitudes and empty promises. He played along for half an hour, then changed tactics.

'How is your grandfather?'

Jason and Nathan Ishikawa exchanged quick glances. 'He's very well. Thank you for asking.'

Alejandro nodded, ignoring the fact that Jason's gaze slid once again to Elise. 'Send him my congratulations on his upcoming seventy-fifth birthday celebrations.'

Nathan cleared his throat. 'We will.' Alejandro waited. The brothers exchanged another glance. 'Until next time, then, Mr Aguilar. *Sayōnara.*' They bowed their heads.

'I look forward to meeting him when I'm in Kyoto soon.'

'You're coming to Japan?' Jason asked.

Alejandro smiled. 'Yours isn't the only deal I'm interested in. I'll have my PA liaise with yours about dates. *Buenos días.*'

He disconnected the call to apprehensive faces.

'I didn't know you had other business interests in Kyoto,' Elise said.

'I don't, but I will by the end of the day. Specifically with Kenzo Ishikawa. Is your passport up to date?'

She frowned. 'Yes, it is. Why?'

'It's time to put your theory to the test. We leave for Kyoto tomorrow morning.'

Elise recognised the luxury town car the moment she stepped out of the similar car Alejandro had sent her home in. They'd worked late into the evening, then he'd spent an hour grilling her on Japanese custom. She was exhausted, but in a good way.

But she'd yet to pack for the trip to Japan and Alejandro was picking her up at 7:00 a.m.

Seeing her mother's lithe, seven-days-a-week-at-the-gym honed body unfold from the back of the car caused her stomach to dip.

And not in a good way.

'You're ignoring my phone calls again.' Marsha Jameson couldn't be accused of beating about the bush. She was dressed to kill in top-to-toe designer clothes and accessories, and not a hair or eyelash deigned to be out of place.

Elise sighed, her grip tightening on her briefcase.

'I'm not. I've been swamped all day. I texted you back to say so.'

Her mother sniffed. 'You know how I feel about texts. If I wanted a text conversation with you, I would've initiated one.'

'I intended to call you when I got home.'

Marsha eyed the apartment block with mild distaste. 'Well, I'm here now.'

Elise raised her eyebrows. 'Would you like to come in?' she invited, torn as to whether she wanted the answer to be yes or no.

'For a minute. I have a pressing engagement in forty-five minutes.'

Ironically, the lifts were downstairs and waiting when they walked in. Elise stepped in, conscious of her mother's gaze, which held its usual disdain as it drifted over her. 'Really, Elise. That grey does nothing for you. And why aren't you wearing any make-up?'

'I am.' She refused to continue applying the unnecessary amount of make-up her mother had insisted she wear in the workplace.

Her mother's eyes narrowed on her face. Thankfully, before she could respond, the lift arrived.

Elise led the way to her door, praying the visit would be quick. But when her mother refused a drink, that pang of hurt made itself very much known.

She sat down on her two-seater while her mother perched on the armchair across from her. Her Realtor had described her apartment as *cute*. Elise knew her parents would have other, far more unsavoury, terms for it.

'I spoke to your grandmother today.'

Elise's stomach dipped further. This house call wasn't about business. 'Right.'

'She told me about the help she's been giving you.'

'Is that a problem?'

'That my mother is helping my daughter do her job? Of course not.' She sniffed. 'I just wanted to make sure you understood that if any help she provides you with doesn't reap the results the client wants, *you're* the one who'll be held responsible.'

Her heart twisted on a fresh wave of pain. 'You don't need to spell it out to me, Mom.'

Hazel-gold eyes the same shade as hers snapped irritation. 'Before you act affronted, I also wanted to say I hope it works out for what you need for SNV.'

Elise's mouth parted in surprise, but her mother wasn't finished. 'I was also alerted by the travel department that you'd requested details of your travel insurance.'

Her mouth snapped shut, the real reason for her mother's visit slowly unfurling. 'Yes. I'm accompanying Al—Mr Aguilar to Kyoto tomorrow.'

The flash of interest in her mother's eyes mildly sickened Elise. 'I thought so. This is excellent news. He obviously thinks very highly of you.'

'Obviously.'

Marsha's gaze hardened. 'Watch your tone, young lady.'

'Prove to me that you didn't drive all the way downtown to dispense the *motherly* advice I think is coming my way, and I will.'

Her mother stared at her for a moment before she shook her head. 'I don't understand you. You've had so many opportunities *handed* to you. And every single time you've turned your nose up at it.'

'Say what you came to say, Mom. Or prove me wrong.'

Her mother's jaw tightened. 'What is so wrong with telling you to make the most of *this* opportunity?'

Pain pierced her. 'The same way you pushed Brian Grey's "opportunity" on me?'

'Don't be ridiculous. That was different.'

'How, Mom? How was it different?' she demanded.

'For starters, Alejandro Aguilar is one of the world's most eligible bachelors. He already sees you as a worthy businesswoman, thanks to your association with Jameson. Capitalise on that and you could become one of the most powerful and iconic women in the world. Of course, I would recommend a trip to a stylist and more care with your hair, but these things can be achieved with a single phone call. Think of what that could mean for Jameson PR. Think of what it could mean for you!'

Blind, foolish tears rushed into Elise's eyes. 'Stop, Mom. Please, just stop.'

'Why? Where's the harm—'

'The *harm* is that I'm not *that* kind of woman! I won't sleep with a man just to get ahead. Alejandro already suspects I'm tarred with the famous Jameson brush!'

Fury surged into her mother's face. But Elise wasn't afraid. Marsha Jameson's fury was the quiet, lethal type. She wasn't prone to ranting or raving. She merely exuded icy rage until the other party deigned to grovel in apology.

But Elise wasn't in the mood to apologise. That need had diminished significantly over the years. Which was not to say the pain that ravaged her insides had abated one iota. In direct contrast to her mother's silent condemnation, her pain howled, long and vicious and deep.

So deep, she barely acknowledged her mother's icy exit.

Elise only rose when she realised her front door had been left wide open. Evidently, Marsha Jameson's anger had no room to accommodate thoughts of her daughter's safety.

After locking the door, Elise went into her bedroom and pulled out her suitcase. The effort not to succumb to tears for the second night in a row nearly failed as she packed. She'd shed enough tears, thanks to fate's decision over her parentage. She was in grave danger of becoming pathetic.

Straightening her spine, she glanced down at the contents of her suitcase. Seeing the greys and blacks tucked inside, she firmed her lips, determinedly zipped the case shut, and tugged it to the front door.

On impulse she pulled out an old, slightly battered flat case. Then immediately swallowed a sob. Adding it to her suitcase, she showered and went to bed. When a tear slipped free, she reassured herself it was for the dream she'd pushed to the back of her life.

A dream that perhaps wouldn't remain a dream for long.

CHAPTER EIGHT

THE RIDE TO Midway International Airport at what felt like the crack of dawn was non-eventful. Unlike the thumping of her heart as the limo Alejandro had sent for her stopped alongside a huge gleaming white private jet with the SNV logo displayed discreetly on the tail.

'Mr Aguilar's already on board, ma'am. Your luggage will be taken care of.' The impeccably uniformed driver doffed his cap after he helped her out.

As she crossed the Tarmac and mounted the steps, her mother's words filtered, unbidden, into her mind. Alejandro indeed commanded a powerful top step on the world stage. Thus far, she'd only experienced him in the environs of his company and very briefly at a dinner that only lasted a few hours.

The swiftness with which he'd secured an audience with Kenzo Ishikawa and started a different set of balls rolling in Kyoto had amazed her yesterday. Stepping into the plane and seeing Alejandro seated at a large conference table, a pile of documents at his elbow, while the crew buzzed around in preparation for the flight, she was suddenly struck by the sheer power he wielded.

Power her mother wanted Elise to whore herself to achieve a slice of.

The brightness of the morning dimmed as despair and desolation threatened to sink deeper into her.

'The quicker you find a seat, the quicker we can take off, Elise.'

She started at the deep drawl. Unwilling to admit what the tenor of that tone did to her see-sawing emotions, she smiled at a crew member who passed her, and made her way across the shockingly spacious midsection to where Alejandro sat. 'Good morning to you, too.'

He lifted a mocking brow at her, and indicated the seat opposite him. '*Buenos días.* If that sour look is because of the early hour, rest assured, you won't be required to work the whole thirteen hours of the flight. There are bedrooms on board. Take a nap, if you feel so inclined.'

Elise shook her head. 'I don't need a nap,' she replied, then promptly yawned.

He sent her a speaking glance. '*Sí,* you're fresh as the proverbial daisy.'

'I slept badly. So sue me.'

He frowned. 'Litigation won't be necessary.

We've all suffered sleepless nights at one point or other.'

'I didn't meant that literally—oh, never mind.'

Tossing his pen onto the table, he sat back and observed her for a full minute before, raising a hand, he summoned an attendant and ordered coffee to be delivered after take-off.

'I'm surprised I didn't realise this before,' he murmured.

'Realise what?'

'You're not a morning person,' he supplied.

Her attempt at a laugh emerged more like a snort. 'Compared to what your idea of morning is, *no one* is a morning person.'

He pressed his fingers into a steeple against his lips, the silky-haired forearms bared by his rolled sleeves flexing in the morning light.

Studiously, Elise averted her gaze from that shockingly sexy display of brawn as the doors were locked and the plane taxied to the runway. She might have condemned her mother for her deplorable suggestions last night, but it didn't mean her insane attraction for Alejandro had dimmed. In fact, his less formal dress and slightly dishevelled hair only added to his intense appeal.

Once they reached cruising altitude, the attendant arrived with a platter of coffee, bagels and croissants. Seizing at the excuse to occupy herself, she grabbed a bagel, then poured and sugared her coffee, before passing Alejandro a cup of espresso.

'*Gracias.*'

When she'd devoured half of the bagel, she glanced at his documents. 'So what do you need me to do?'

'I meant what I said. You don't need to work during the flight.'

She frowned. 'I'm supposed to twiddle my thumbs for thirteen hours?'

'I'm attempting to be less…ogre-tastic, Elise. Take advantage of it.'

The words were too similar to those she'd heard a few short hours ago. As absurd as it was, they struck a chord of disquiet. She didn't want to take advantage of anything or anyone. 'I'd rather not,' she bit out.

'Why do I get the feeling I've misstepped?'

A quick investigative glance showed his incisive gaze on her. Elise shook her head, hoping to dispel his interest, but he carried on looking at her.

'It's not important. Seriously,' she stressed when his eyes narrowed.

After a moment he nodded, and returned his attention to his documents. A full hour passed before she lost the battle to stay still. With nothing for her to do but leaf through mindless magazines, her attention continued to stray to Alejandro. The pen he twirled through his fingers became a source of fascination. As did the drift of his fingers down the surface of his tablet.

Enough already.

Looking around, she smiled at the attendant who caught her eye. When he started towards her, she rose from her seat.

And gasped when Alejandro's hand closed over her wrist. 'Need something?'

She attempted to speak, despite the heat travelling up her arm. 'I...yes. I'm not sure how the luggage thing works on private jets. I'm wondering whether I can get access to my stuff. No problem if not...'

Without letting go of her, Alejandro rose to tower over her. 'Your things were stowed in one of the bedrooms. I'll show you.' A jerk of his head dismissed the attendant. Heading to the back of the plane, he indicated a short flight of stairs.

She'd erred on the side of not too casual but with travel comfort in mind when she chose the navy flared skirt and white short-sleeved shirt she was wearing. But now as she went up the stairs she wondered whether her skirt was too short, her shirt a little too clingy.

Hating herself for letting her mother's views seep

into her confidence, she headed towards the single door at the top level and opened it. The bedroom was larger than her apartment's, with a king-size bed draped in cotton sheets and a blood-red coverlet. On the opposite wall, a high-tech entertainment and drinks centre stood beneath a wide-screen TV, with a dove-grey velvet-covered chaise longue set against one wall. Next to the chaise, she spotted an open closet where her suitcase and art bag had been stashed next to another set of suitcases.

The space was undoubtedly designed for relaxation, but it was the *sort* of relaxation that had Elise's breath snagging in her chest and her pulse racing at a frenetic pace.

She heard the door shut behind her and turned. 'I'll just grab my stuff and go back down.'

He walked towards her, his pace predatorily graceful in a way that made her want to watch him for a very long time. 'Why?' he asked, as if her question was absurd in the extreme.

'I get the feeling… Is this your bedroom?' she blurted.

'*Sí.* It's the quietest place on the airplane, thanks to great soundproofing. You won't be disturbed here.'

But *he* was disturbing her with his scent, his body and the banked heat emanating from his eyes.

'I really just want to grab one thing—'

'You have shadows under your eyes, Elise. Shadows that weren't there last night despite the events of the past couple of days. I need you on top of your game by the time we land. So rest. I insist.' He went to the bed and pulled down the covers. Grasping one pillow, he fluffed it.

The sight of his manly bronze fingers against the white sheet was so shockingly erotic, Elise felt a clenching between her thighs. Locking her knees, she held her breath as he strolled back to her. His forefinger traced the skin beneath her eyes for several heartbeats before he dropped his hand.

'There's a buzzer next to the bed that summons an attendant. Use it when you wake up if you need anything. Lunch will be delivered to you if you wish, or you can come downstairs.'

'Okay. Thanks.'

He was gone in quick, silent strides. The breath expelled from her lungs in a rush, her heart hammering as if she'd run a marathon.

Walking to the chaise, she sat and dragged a hand down her face. Heaven help her, whatever this fevered sensation was that came over her whenever Alejandro was near, she needed to find a solution to it, and quickly, before she made a fool of herself.

Or worse, confirmed his 'like mother, like daughter' indictment.

The thought sent a cold shiver through her, dispelling a little of the hot tingles shooting through her body.

Rising, she went to the closet and picked up the extra bag she'd packed last night.

She hadn't touched her art supplies in years. Elise wasn't exactly sure why she'd packed it, or why she imagined she'd find solace in her art now when her every attempt in the last few years had felt forced and stilted. But ever since divulging the existence of her art degree to Alejandro, she'd felt a growing need to revisit her discarded dream. To see if, *this* time, it would speak to her.

Kicking off her shoes, she settled on the bed and set up the collapsible easel before her.

Her heart leapt into her throat as she scrolled through the pages of her sketchbook, revisiting abandoned stories. What if she could never reclaim this lifeline? Her manga creations were what had sustained her through her teenage years. Would they sustain her now? She turned the pages back and read through old sketches, trying to pull herself back into the story.

Half an hour later, her fingers were still poised

over a blank sheet. A thread of fear feathered her nape. Had she lost her muse for ever?

Elise forced herself to breathe. Eyes shut, she traced the pencil over the blank sheet. She knew the subject of her sketch the moment her fingers began to move.

Almost trancelike, she sketched Alejandro's profile. Proud and regal, the image of him staring out of his office window at the view of Lake Michigan felt so real, her fingers trembled as she traced the fine lines, lingering with almost sinful delight over the curve of his lips. He was out of bounds to her for many reasons. But there was no reason she couldn't have this.

Except *this* was a dangerous pastime, one she couldn't afford to indulge in unless she wanted to invite a whole new set of problems for herself. She finished Alejandro's sketch and returned to her manga story. The first image appeared within minutes.

Relief punched through her as the next image unfolded, followed by another.

Elise worked until her muscles grew stiff and her eyes began to droop. Setting aside the papers and easel with a deep sense of awe and accomplishment, she released the clip from her hair, and slid down into the comfortable bed. The ironic thought that the man she was so desperate to keep her guard up around was the same one who'd turned out to be her creative muse was the last she had as the hum of the plane lulled her into a floating sleep.

Only to be awaked by a wildly jarring movement.

Blinking, she sat up. The shades on the windows had been pulled halfway down, and a soft lamp turned low, leaving the room in a golden glow.

In the chaise, Alejandro sat nursing a cognac.

'Uh…hi,' she murmured.

Intense eyes drifted to her as he took a sip. 'I left the light on so you wouldn't think I'm sitting here in the dark watching you sleep like some sort of creep,' he drawled.

His presence was inducing a myriad of feelings, but creepiness wasn't one of them.

She licked her lower lip and surreptitiously smoothed her hair. 'How long have I been asleep?'

'Five hours. I imagine you would've slept for longer had we not flown into turbulence. The pilot tells me it'll go on for a while. I thought you might appreciate a friendly face in case you're a timid flyer,' he mocked gently.

Her gaze darted to the windows, although there wasn't much to see. She shrugged. 'I'm the no-point-in-panicking-until-there's-something-to-*really*-panic-about type of flyer.'

He smiled into his drink. 'How fatalistic of you.' Rising, he crossed to the bar and poured a mineral water. Elise tried to avert her gaze as he headed for her, but her eyes refused to cooperate. Breathless once more, she watched him advance with a lithe, powerful prowl.

As he held out the water the plane bounced again, spilling it onto her outstretched hand. Alejandro placed the glass on the bedside table, grabbed a tissue and dabbed drops from her hand, his eyes on her face the whole time.

'Not as many shadows. I trust you slept better than you did last night?'

The deep timbre of his voice vibrated through her. 'Yes. Thanks for offering me your bed.'

Nice, Elise. Fighting not to cringe or blush, she started to reach for the water.

The plane bounced again.

Glancing at the distance between the top of Alejandro's head and the low ceiling, she smirked. 'Maybe you should sit down before your head makes a hole in the ceiling and you doom us all?'

His mouth twitched as he perched at the foot of the bed. 'You seem in a better mood, too.' His gaze flicked to the zipped-up portfolio case that held her drawings. 'Does this have something to do with it?'

She tensed slightly, unable to stem the ingrained

wariness about her art. When his eyes reflected nothing but genuine interest, she nodded. 'It hasn't for a while but it helped today, yes.'

He nodded, his gaze resting speculatively on the case. When it flicked back to her, her heart tripped.

'Are you going to make me beg to see them, Elise?' he murmured.

Her fingers toyed with a corner of the sheet, her nerves jumping in time to the turbulence. 'I don't know…maybe?'

Eyes gleaming with intent traced her face before reconnecting with hers. '*Por favor.* I would be honoured to see your art.'

She grimaced. 'Damn. You don't play fair.'

A ghost of a smile curved his mouth. 'No. I don't.'

She reached for the case to extract her sketchbook, an absurd part of her acknowledging she would be totally crushed if he didn't like it. Calling herself all kinds of a fool, she held it out to him.

Alejandro opened it. Surprise flickered in his eyes, then both eyebrows gradually spiked with each page he perused. Finally, when she didn't think she would be able to stand the tension, he raised his head. '*Que están más allá de magnífica,*' he rasped.

'Translation, please,' she whispered.

'Magnificent.'

Pleasure shot through her, her smile powered by a thousand bulbs of happiness. 'Thank you.'

He stared at her for a beat before returning his attention to the pages. 'This is what you intend to do when you're done with Jameson?'

'It's what I've wanted to do for a long time, but...'

'But?'

'I was afraid I'd lost...something. My work has felt stilted for a long time now.'

He regarded her steadily. 'You had other things on your mind.'

Slowly she nodded. 'Yes.'

Deft fingers leafed through the pages with escalating speed. 'And your parents have a problem with *this*?'

Her fist knotted on the sheet. 'My parents have a problem with most things I do. Or more accurately, what I *don't*—' She bit her tongue to stop words she didn't want to spill.

His head lifted from the pages, green eyes narrowed. 'What do they want?'

She shook her head. 'I'd prefer not to—'

'Your talent is undeniable. So tell me why they'd choose not to support you,' he pressed.

'Do your parents support you in everything you do?'

His face froze, a darkly forbidding look blanketing his features. 'We're not talking about me.'

'Answer my question and I'll answer yours.'

For a long minute, she thought he wouldn't respond. 'I haven't sought my parents' approval and they haven't been in a position to give it because I haven't spoken to them in almost fifteen years,' he clipped out. 'Now you.'

Elise closed the mouth that had dropped open and tried to stem the rising dread. 'I don't like talking about them.'

His jaw tensed for a second. 'Because I erroneously likened you to them?'

The plane jarred her stomach into free fall for a second but her gaze didn't leave his face. 'Maybe. You have me as your captive audience at thirty-four thousand feet. Tell me what you'd have said differently.'

'I wouldn't have thrown your parents' reputation in your face, for a start. I, more than anyone, should know that genetically we're formed from their blueprints, but we're not the sum total of our parents' beliefs and actions.'

A sudden lump in her throat made it hard to breathe or speak. She tried anyway. 'I... Thanks.' She swallowed. Then realised he was waiting for more. 'They think I'm not making the most of my... assets.'

He tensed. 'Your assets,' he breathed.

'You want to know why I smile at everyone I meet?'

His eyes gleamed dangerously. 'Not particularly, but go on.'

'Because at seventeen, my mother told me that *not* smiling would make me more mysterious and attractive to men. That I would have them falling at my feet if I maintained a certain…aloofness. I've been getting advice like that since I hit puberty. After what happened with Brian, I wondered for a while if they'd been right.' She laughed bitterly. 'I even wondered whether I'd invited the assault.'

He captured her nape so fast, her breath stalled. *'You did not,'* he said through clenched teeth. 'That was all him. Never think otherwise.'

She nodded jerkily, her chest tightening with the intensity of him.

After a moment, he relaxed and released her. Lounging back on the bed, he regarded her. 'So you decided to smile because you didn't wish to have men falling at your feet?'

She grimaced. 'That sounds ludicrous, I know. They can fall all they want. I'd just prefer they wait two seconds and engage my intellect before they decide I'm worth falling for. Besides, all those potentially falling bodies to navigate? If I wanted that, I'd have trained as a stuntwoman.'

His low laugh dispelled the knot in her midriff, and promptly replaced it with a glow. 'That would be a sight to behold.'

She smiled. 'Thankfully, you'll never have to see it. I'm not built for that profession, either.'

His gaze lingered for a heartbeat, before raking down her body. 'At the risk of being called a chauvinist, I won't divulge my thoughts on what you're built for.'

She pressed her lips together to stop herself from demanding he tell her. Because the heat swirling in his eyes wasn't dangerous enough!

But he looked down. Started to turn the page.

'Wait!' Elise lunged forward.

His breath audibly caught.

The plane lurched, throwing her into an awkward sprawl next to him. He caught and steadied her with one hand, his other holding the page open. The page that held his image. Silence, thick and heavy, hung in the room.

Elise tried to move. He held her still, his gaze rising to hers.

'This is how you see me?' he rasped after an interminable age. His voice was completely devoid of emotion, depriving her of any insight as to how he felt about the drawing.

She swallowed hard. 'I… Yes.'

Unreadable eyes dropped to the image again, prompting hers to follow. 'I look...'

'Angry. Sad. Lonely. Invincible.'

'*Dios*. Why did you draw it?' he demanded roughly.

'I don't know.'

'Yes, you do. Why?' he pressed.

'I couldn't concentrate...because you were on my mind?'

'Is that a question? Either I was or I wasn't.'

She was aware she was skirting that edge of danger she'd craved mere minutes ago. Her blood thrummed wildly in her ears. 'You were. Very much.'

He roughly shoved the case aside and pulled her fully into his body.

His fingers speared into her hair, his grip firm as he leaned down and stared, narrow-eyed, at her.

'You know why I'm angry.'

'The deal. Your brother. Yes.'

His nostrils flared. 'I'm not sad.'

'Maybe not right this minute.'

He made a rough sound of disagreement. 'I'm *not* lonely,' he rasped.

Her heart lurched, because the evidence to the contrary was right there in his voice. 'Okay.'

'My invincibility would be debated by some.'

'But only if they're blind?'

He shrugged. His head dropped another fraction. 'This picture… You see too much, Elise. I don't like it.'

'You see me, too, when you want to, but you don't see me throwing a tantrum about it.'

His eyes darkened. The fingers in her hair shifted, caressed. *'Madre de Dios.'*

Desire dripped into her veins, commencing a slow languor that held her captive and yearning.

She needed to pull back, retreat to her side of the bed. Or better still, out of the room completely. 'Alejandro…'

'Shut up. I've had quite enough words from you for now.'

His mouth slanted over hers, mastered her, showed her the depth of feeling moving through him. She didn't need words to know her drawing had affected him. The way he kissed, with hunger and a little anger, need and a touch of gentleness, told its own story.

Drugging enough to make her momentarily excuse herself from what shouldn't be happening; she explored him with the same hunger. Beneath her fingers, his warm muscles shifted, the hair at his nape curled into her touch, his whole body shuddering when her nails dug in.

'Elise.'

He lifted his head for a moment and she glimpsed the powerful hunger stamped on his face. It was enough to remind her that she was playing with fire. That she was stoking an inferno she might not be able to survive if it flamed much higher.

Before she could attempt to push him away, he was kissing her again, bearing her back so she was flat on the bed.

One hand traced her jaw, then stroked down to linger at the pulse beating at her throat. When he was satisfied she was sufficiently fired up, he trailed lower, and cupped one breast.

Elise moaned at the expert kneading, the clever teasing of her nipple. Liquid sensation sparked through her, singeing her between the legs until she was twisting beneath him. He uttered something guttural in Spanish, intensely erotic.

The plane lurched, separating them for a second. They stared at each other. Awareness slowly crawled back. They'd been here before.

And yet here she was, thousands of feet in the air, on the edge of being initiated into an exclusive club with a man who would sign her paycheque when her business with him was over and walk away without a backward glance.

He started to lower his head.

She pulled away. 'No.'

He exhaled harshly. 'We've been here before. I misjudged you then. I'm not doing it now.'

She forced her hands to drop from his shoulders. 'Thank you, but nothing has changed. I can't do this.' Her lips were stiff, as if they didn't want to speak the words.

A frown formed. 'I've spent more than two seconds with you. I've engaged your intelligence.'

'So now you're ready to fall at my feet?' she parried.

His features slid into neutral. 'I don't fall, Elise. Ever.'

Something jarred hard and cold inside her. 'And I don't sleep with people I work with.'

'Who *do* you sleep with?' he queried tersely.

'Not that it's any of your business, but I haven't. Ever.'

One mocking eyebrow lifted. 'You expect me to believe you're a virgin?'

Heat stormed up her face in evidence before she could utter a word. Something akin to shock paled his face.

'Elise—'

'I'm not having this conversation with you. Believe what you will, but do it while you're not lying on top of me.'

He released her immediately, his movements jerky as he retreated.

She averted her gaze from him, slid off the bed, stood, and attempted to straighten her embarrassingly wrinkled clothes.

They both startled when the intercom buzzed and the pilot announced they would be free of the turbulence in a few minutes.

Elise almost snorted. The turbulence in her life had taken the form of a powerful and enigmatic man whose compulsive power drew her inexorably in as every instinct screamed for her to run in the other direction. She might have succeeded in stopping her emotions from unravelling completely a few moments ago, but Elise feared she wouldn't be as strong should any further turmoil be hurled her way.

Until she could finish her job and walk away, her only option was to distance herself as much as possible from Alejandro.

CHAPTER NINE

OF COURSE THAT was easier said than done.

From the moment they landed, she found herself in the very close and personal position of being Alejandro's interpreter.

In between a whirlwind tour of Kyoto with her, he shamelessly courted Ishikawa Corporation's rivals.

He accepted a meeting with the Ishikawa brothers two days after landing, which he then cancelled at the last minute with profuse apologies.

'You're taunting them,' Elise observed as they stood beneath one of hundreds of red arches that lined the pathway to Fushimi Inari-taisha Shrine. They'd paused halfway on the two-hour trek to the top, and, beneath them, Kyoto glistened resplendently in the evening light.

Elise breathed in deep, her heart lifting with a serenity she hadn't felt for a long time.

Each morning since their arrival three days ago, Alejandro had instructed her to pick a place to visit. Their first visit had been to the Kiyomizu-dera temple close to where her grandmother lived. Her grandmother might have been absent but she'd arranged a private visit of the holy temple renowned for bestowing good fortune and love. As they'd strolled through the hallowed room, Elise had told herself the latter hadn't been why she'd chosen the temple as her first port of call. Her heart had twanged with disbelief, but she'd shoved the feeling aside. Alejandro had strolled beside her with ease, pointing out scrolls he needed translating, then looking at her with blatant heat as she read them out to him in Japanese, then translated.

In those moments, she'd asked herself whether she was taking her reticence a little too far. Whether she wasn't risking throwing away a spell of ecstasy for a lifetime of the unknown.

She glanced at him now as he traced his fingers down the scrolls on the arch. He turned, and one of the incisive gazes he'd taken to levelling on her since their turbulent and very eye-opening conversation on the plane bore into her.

She'd told herself she preferred things this way—looks without touching or any hint of the emotional and physical intimacy they'd shared on the plane. But slowly those feelings were changing.

'Giving them a taste of their own medicine,' Alejandro responded to her question.

She walked from one scroll to the next, her breath

catching when he followed. 'You know your brother's here in Kyoto. What if they decide to go with him?'

He shrugged. 'Then I would've lost.'

Elise frowned. 'After all the effort you put in?'

A distant look entered his eyes. 'This is a battle I never wished to be drawn into in the first place. Winning at all costs may appear romantic on the big screen, but I've never been a fan of pyrrhic victories.'

She gazed up at him. 'What about compromises? Are you a fan of those?'

Narrowed green eyes speared hers. 'Explain.'

'Have you thought about sitting down with your brother and hashing this out?'

His mouth firmed. 'It won't work.'

'Why not? Because you tried before?'

'No.'

'Alejandro—'

'Leave it alone, Elise.'

Her gaze dropped for a second. 'You both want the same thing. Has it occurred to you that you can have it if you relent a little bit?'

His jaw clenched. 'I don't do well with family. I never have. I never will.'

She knew she ought to let it go, but the words

poured out nevertheless. 'You didn't do well *in the past*. But now you've met Gael again—'

'For a handful of minutes in my office.'

'Bite my head off if you want, but I've seen you two together. You can salvage this if you would just—'

'*Basta!* Enough.' He linked his hand through hers and started up the slope of the shrine. Elise fell silent, partly because their surroundings were too beautiful to spoil with an argument. And partly because she liked him holding her hand. A little too much.

Later that afternoon, he stood looking out onto the lotus-flowered landscape beyond the window.

The resort was situated north of Kyoto, built beside a meandering river and extending from a central villa said to have once been the private residence of an emperor. Its natural beauty was stunning and the contemporary design blended with traditional floor-level seats and indigenous decorations.

But she didn't see any of that beauty now, her attention absorbed wholly by Alejandro.

He sensed her behind him and turned. Her heart lurched at the contemplative look on his face.

'About our earlier conversation. I don't know why you think you know enough about me to present these opinions,' he drawled, his tone gruff. 'But let me give you a brief background about us before you think playing happy families is in any way an option for us.'

'I didn't say that—'

'Gael is a product of an affair my father had with his mother when I was three years old. When I was old enough, I found out there'd been affairs before I was born, and my father had no intention of stopping after I came along. But Gael's mother was the most...turbulent of all, probably because she was the only woman who managed to convince my father to leave my mother. And he did. For a short time, at least. He went to play happy families with Gael's mother. Gael was born, and then suddenly my father was back home. My mother hated herself for taking him back. To her, his previous affairs had been meaningless and easily overlooked.

'But it was different with Gael's mother. Perversely, she felt as if he'd broken her trust. They fought day and night. You know what it's like living with a parent who falls apart every time my father is five minutes late coming home? You know how many times she dragged me from my bed and into the car so she could go in search of him to make sure he wasn't in another woman's bed? Gael's mother did that to my family.' He turned from the window, prowling across the floor until he stood before her. 'Do you think, coming from *that*, that there can be any peace between us?'

'I'm sure Gael didn't exactly escape unscathed, either.'

'I *know*,' he breathed, shaking his head. 'But when you're caught in this...*powder keg*, rationality goes out of the window.'

Let it go, Elise. Your own family situation is far from a bundle of laughs. Let it—

'That was then, Alejandro. What about now?'

He shook his head. 'It's too late.'

'I don't think so.'

His expression underwent a subtle transformation. Elise was willing to bet he didn't know how vulnerable he'd looked for just a second before his features hardened. 'Don't presume to know how to fix me, Elise.'

'I wouldn't dare. I'm only stating the obvious. I can shut up if you want me to?'

He stared at her, narrow-eyed, for a second. 'I don't want you to shut up. But this subject bores me. So change it, if you please.'

She grimaced. 'Well, we've done the tourist thing, the business thing. We've made a mockery of family. What shall we do next?'

His gaze dropped to her mouth, but he didn't

speak. He didn't need to. The look on his face told its own unfolding story, morphing from chillingly forbidding to stark raving hunger.

One hand snagged her waist. The heat in his eyes was back, full force. 'Sex, Elise. Let's do sex. And don't give me the excuse about our working relationship or you not wanting me. We can make this work. The day after we first kissed, you walked back into my office and carried on working even though my behaviour was less than exemplary. You didn't throw a tantrum or give me the cold shoulder like most women I know would've done. I have no doubt that whatever happens between us in the bedroom, it will not get in the way of your job.'

She tried to speak past the sudden clamouring of her senses. Tried to *think*. 'Wow. I sound like a robot.'

His mouth quirked, but his gaze didn't lose one ounce of intensity. 'If you were, you'd be the sexiest one ever created.'

Laughter barked from her, which he joined in with for a few seconds, before the sexual gravity of the moment rendered them both silent.

'I want you, Elise. You might not wish to reciprocate the statement right now, but let's agree to table it for discussion after Kenzo Ishikawa's birthday party tomorrow, *sí*?'

The past few days had been leading to this. Somewhere along the line, she'd decided to take the chance. But now he was laying out terms so starkly, her senses shrieked a primal warning. 'Alejandro, I don't know...'

'Come on now, we've tried to pretend this isn't happening, but it is. You can't keep running from it and I don't intend to fail the challenge and pleasure of getting you into my bed. You have twenty-four hours to yield to me. And, Elise?'

'Yes?' she murmured despite her spinning thoughts.

'I don't intend to lose this one.'

A hard kiss preceded his exit.

Elise dropped into the chair, her stunned senses trying to grapple with what had just happened.

Alejandro had dropped a giant morsel of his past in her lap. Then segued into a demand for sex. She stared at the door through which he'd disappeared. Was the instigation of the subject of sex a way to distract her from his emotional revelations?

If so, it'd worked a treat.

Skirting past the momentous subject of sex with Alejandro, she replayed his childhood story instead.

She'd thought her childhood had been horrendous with the early realisation that her parents had what amounted to an open marriage, their vows shoved into the background in the interest of accumulating financial gain. For the greater part, Elise had been handed over to the care of nannies and housekeepers while her parents pursued their single-minded interests. It hadn't been until she hit puberty that things had changed for the worse.

Alejandro's experiences had been worse, because the infidelity had come from one side, with pain heaped on his mother while he'd been caught in the middle.

She might not have heard Gael's side, or know the full story, but what little she knew explained the brief glimpses of bleakness and loneliness she sometimes saw in Alejandro's eyes.

Her heart squeezed in sympathy and despite telling herself that softening her feelings for him might be a dangerous path to take, she still found herself mourning long into the evening and into the night for the harrowing childhood he must have suffered.

As for the subject of sex, she continued to push it to the back of her mind whenever it sparked its heady temptation. She knew not confronting it wouldn't make it go away—she'd seen a determined Alejandro in action, after all—but all the same, she held it at bay, in the hope that morning would bring the clarity she needed.

CHAPTER TEN

SHE WAS STILL set on resisting him.

Alejandro knew this from the small frown knotting her brow. She wouldn't succeed. Having Elise Jameson in his bed had swept beyond a lustful, persistent want, into a primeval need. One he didn't intend to deny himself.

The subject of her virginity—if it was true—unsettled him somewhat. Then again, everything about Elise was turning out to be uncharted territory for him.

She got under his skin in the most disturbing way, but not enough for him to step back from the clamouring desire raging through his blood. Perhaps, once he'd had her, she would cease to have this peculiar power over him.

He *would* have her.

But for now he had other matters to deal with.

'My grandmother received your flowers,' Elise said. Her frown momentarily disappeared, a hint of the smile that toyed with his breathing when in full bloom curving her lightly glossed lips. 'She called when I was getting dressed. She wanted to thank you. She says to tell you they're the most beautiful flowers she's ever received.'

His own mouth curved. 'She was the perfect absent hostess and she ensured our invitation to Kenzo Ishikawa's birthday party. It was the least I could do.'

Her smile widened. 'She did say you owe her big, though. And that she might call in her chips when you least expect it.'

'I look forwarding to meeting her one day. She sounds formidable.'

Pride propelled her nod. 'She's one of the strongest people I know. She's the product of a Pearl Harbour love story that almost didn't happen.' Her smile slipped a little. 'Her childhood was rough. When it was her turn to become a mother, she tried to shield my mother as much as possible. She believes she overcompensated by spoiling my mother, which is why…' She shook her head and stopped.

Alejandro reached for her hand. It was an unfamiliar offer of comfort, and yet it felt right. 'You reminded me that the apple sometimes *does* fall far enough from the tree to seek its own roots and light. Your mother may have been spoilt as a child, but I doubt the grandmother who encouraged you to follow your dreams also encouraged your mother to take the particular path she's taken. I bet they disagree on a few things?'

'They disagree on everything! They fought constantly about the way she was bringing me up. My grandmother couldn't bear it any longer, which is why she moved back to Hawaii. Surprisingly, they have a better relationship now they're thousands of miles apart.'

'Distance provides clarity. Sometimes.'

She eyed him, and Alejandro knew what was coming. 'Did it do that for you?' she asked.

Surprisingly, her question didn't grate on him. Although the chafing layer of disquiet closely resembling guilt and regret that had manifested when Gael visited him in his office intensified.

He shifted in his seat. 'It taught me that I never wanted to be in that situation. I've seen the wedding pictures. I've heard the stories of how they met. My parents married believing they were happy. For some reason, that changed very soon afterwards. They took pleasure in hurting one another until they were locked so fully into their macabre roles they couldn't see anything or anyone else, not even their son. I knew very early, I wanted nothing to do with that level of emotional turbulence.'

She looked pensive. 'True compatibility in any relationship is hard to find, I know, but just because that happened to them doesn't mean it'll happen to you.'

'It didn't just happen to me. It happened to Gael. It happened to his mother. It happened to everyone my parents came into contact with. The Aguilar brain may be good for business, but there's no heart there to sustain meaningful relationships. I accepted that a long time ago.'

Her eyes shadowed, her face losing colour.

'What's wrong?' he asked.

She averted her face sharply towards the window. 'Nothing. I'm fine.'

Alejandro let it go, but he wondered if his declaration had been too harsh.

But the truth often was. Realising his parents had no room in their life for him had hurt for a long time. Time and distance had dulled the pain. Increasingly fleeting liaisons, which proved he wasn't built for relationships, had only confirmed his suspicions.

He was more than content to accept the status quo.

Except the regret continues to chafe...

The hand within his grip moved. He gripped it tighter. As he stared down at their entwined hands something moved through him. Something numinous that had nothing to do with the electric heat of their touching palms.

The emotion further unsettled him. So much so, when the limo driving them to Ishikawa's party drew to a stop at the top of a small hill, relief poured through him. Alighting, he took a deep, sustaining gulp of the cool evening air.

All around cherry blossoms flowered in pinks, reds and whites. Spring in Kyoto was breathtaking. But nothing surpassed the beauty of the woman who stepped out beside him a second later.

His gaze moved over her, quiet satisfaction eroding some of the tumult.

He'd called in a stylist when she'd asked for time off to go shopping. Her clear embarrassment and distress had made him probe deeper, which had led to the discovery that she hadn't packed adequately due to a visit from her mother.

She hadn't needed to go into great detail for him to know her mother was the reason she'd boarded his plane with shadows under her eyes. Those shadows were gone now. He paused to appreciate her feminine form in a red gown that bared her shoulders and warmed her complexion, the lightly made-up face and elegantly styled hair.

Alejandro decided then and there that he would encourage her to wear more red. Especially in bed.

Drawing back from anticipatory carnal pleasures before he succumbed to the urge to hustle her back into the car and to their hotel room, he offered his arm.

She readily accepted it, a fact that pleased him greatly.

Kenzo Ishikawa's birthday party was being held in a converted Japanese temple on the grounds of the Ishikawa private estate. The structure was a replica of the world-renowned Golden Pavilion, and, like its namesake, golden light poured from wide windows and spilled onto the man-made lake surrounding the structure.

Alejandro escorted Elise across a wooden bridge and they were met with barefooted geishas, serving champagne and canapés. He handed her a glass and took one for himself, but Alejandro wasn't interested in drinking.

He spotted his brother from across the room and acknowledged Gael's stiff greeting with one of his own. Then a well-dressed old man with a walking stick heading their way drew his attention.

Setting his glass down, he held out his hand. 'Mr Ishikawa-san, thank you for inviting us to your party,' Alejandro said. 'Allow me to introduce you—'

'No introduction needed, Mr Aguilar. Elise's

grandmother is a good friend of mine, and is quite adept at twisting my arm when it suits her,' Kenzo replied dryly, his shrewd eyes lingering on Elise for a moment before returning to Alejandro.

'We're honoured to be here,' Elise replied, her smile warm as she gave a small bow. She handed over the oblong ribbon-tied present. 'A gift from my grandmother.'

The old man's snowy brows lifted. 'More gifts? I received yours this afternoon, Mr Aguilar. Along with your note.'

Alejandro nodded. 'Twenty minutes of your time later, if you would be so kind.'

Kenzo's dark eyes regarded him steadily. 'That is twice longer than your brother requested.'

Alejandro's kept his expression neutral. 'Then between us we won't take up too much of your time.'

The old man watched him with eyes that saw too much. 'Did you not consider it expedient to speak to me *together*?' he replied.

The chafing reasserted itself, rubbing harsh and relentless. 'The timing isn't quite right.'

Kenzo nodded, his expression holding an understanding that jarred Alejandro. 'Of course. Timing. The one thing we all wish we were experts at.' Before Alejandro could respond, he turned to Elise.

'Would you accompany me to my seat, my dear? I'd love to hear what you've been up to since I last spoke to your grandmother.'

Elise sent Alejandro a wary glance. He didn't want to let her go. The realisation wasn't surprising. After all, hadn't the days since the incident on his plane been revelatory in many ways? He desired her. But he was drawn to her in other ways besides sexually. He wasn't quite ready yet to explore those other emotions. But somewhere along the way an acceptance of his suddenly possessive disposition had settled in.

'Alejandro?'

He focused on her stunning face, realised he was still holding on to her and released her. '*Sí*. Of course. I'll see you later.'

Her wariness didn't abate, but she nodded. Vowing to address it at the first opportunity, he watched her walk away, her revived smile luminescent enough to draw glances as she made her way through the crowded room.

'*Madre de Dios*. If beauty like hers could be bottled, I'd be a hell of a lot richer than I am right now,' Gael drawled from beside him. 'Things are still platonic between you two, right? So you won't mind if I ask her out—'

'She's off limits to you, Gael,' Alejandro snarled. The icy fury that scoured through him at the very thought of Gael with Elise was shocking in the extreme. 'For your own sake, don't make me repeat myself on this subject. Ever.'

Gael held up his hands in mock surrender, a low laugh accompanying the gesture. 'Okay, okay. *Basta de charla!*' Enough said.

Alejandro exhaled, unclenching fists he hadn't realised he'd balled. When another champagne server approached, he grabbed a glass, just for something to do with his hands.

'Are you always this wound up? It can't be good for your health,' Gael muttered, sipping his own drink.

'My health is none of your concern,' he snapped.

Gael's face closed up. 'Of course. Trust me, you made that pretty clear in Chicago.'

The emotions eating at him suddenly multiplied, sapping his control. 'This may be a party, but I'm here for business only. If you're seeking me out under the misapprehension that it would be anything else, you're about to be sorely disappointed.'

A grim smile touched Gael's lips. 'And does that statement apply to everyone here, or just me?'

'What are you talking about?' he demanded, yearning for something, *anything* to help end this conversation. With an unstoppable compulsion, he sought out Elise.

She was at Kenzo's table, with the old man and his grandsons surrounding her. Alejandro watched as Jason Ishikawa leaned over and whispered in her ear. She laughed, her face so beautiful. His breath caught.

'Nothing. Forget it,' Gael murmured.

Alejandro barely heard him leave. Jealousy pounded, strong and hot through him as he watched her interact with the younger Ishikawa brother.

As if sensing his regard, she lifted her head. Her expression dimmed, escalating his suspicion that something was wrong.

Something he'd said to her in the car had upset her. But what?

Go to her. Find out. Claim her.

No. She needed to be handled with care. If she was as innocent as he was beginning to believe she was, the way he was feeling right now would cause more harm than good. She wasn't a fragile creature by any means, but neither was she equipped to handle the riotous emotions surging through his veins. She'd already borne the brunt of his jealousy on more than one occasion.

He needed to calm down a little…*or a lot*, before he tackled anything further with her.

He mingled. He sipped vintage champagne. He forced himself not to react each time Jason whispered in her ear.

Alejandro turned away, knowing he was one heartbeat from ripping Jason Ishikawa from her side. He swallowed his ire, torturously reined in his fraying control, and mingled for an hour until the traditional dinner gong sounded.

'Alejandro?'

Her voice lanced through him, touched him places he couldn't quite name. Turning from the female acquaintance who'd sought him out under the pretext of discussing business only to shoot him interest-filled looks the moment they were alone, he glanced at Elise.

'Are you ready to be seated?' she asked.

'*Sí*. Are you?' he enquired, refusing to glance in Jason Ishikawa's direction.

Her eyes skated away from him, but her smile stayed in place. 'Yes.'

'Then come.' Dismissing the acquaintance with a stiff smile, he held out his arm.

She hesitated. Dread snapped up his spine.

'Something wrong?' he asked as they neared their table.

'Is there any reason it should be?' she tossed back.

'You're answering my questions with questions. Is this a prelude to an argument, *guapa*?'

She swallowed. 'I don't know what you're talking—'

'Mr Aguilar, my grandfather would be honoured if you and Elise would consider joining us at our table.'

Alejandro faced Jason Ishikawa, every nerve in his body yearning to refuse the invitation. In fact, right then, he wanted to call a halt to everything: the merger that had dominated his life up to only a handful of days ago but was now a load he wanted to shed. The brother whose weighted gaze he could even now feel upon him… Everything, just so he could walk out of the party with Elise.

But leaving would be a gross insult not just to her and her grandmother, but also to their hosts. So he gritted his teeth and nodded his acceptance.

A few feet from the table, he noticed Gael had also been relocated. And Elise was placed beside Kenzo, with his grandsons on either side of them.

The old man had an agenda of his own, one Alejandro wasn't certain of yet. But he would play along. For now.

He'd come to Kyoto with the intention of saving the merger, but no deal was worth mind games or further interminable delays if they meant not having Elise in his bed. He would leave here tonight with the merger agreed. Or he would not.

It was that simple.

Decision made, he allowed himself to enjoy the food, the drink, and his immediate companions. For his own state of mind, he chose to ignore the overt gestures Jason made towards Elise. She would be leaving here with him, not Jason. And after tonight, there would be no doubt in her mind that she was his. He would make sure she understood that attention from other men wouldn't be tolerated.

Once dinner was over, he sat back as Gael invited a female guest to the dance floor. Elise excused herself to the bathroom and the Ishikawa brothers went off to fulfil their hosting duties.

He wasn't surprised when Kenzo stood and gestured for Alejandro to walk with him.

They stepped out into the balmy late-April evening, Kenzo's steps slow but steady as they took a meandering path that led to a smaller, well-lit pagoda surrounded by stone statues.

Inside, the old man selected a seat, indicating the one opposite him. Once Alejandro sat, he said, 'Speak, son.'

'You know why I'm here.'

'You think I'm the one getting in the way of the merger?'

'I just want straight answers.'

Kenzo nodded. 'Very well. You're a lone wolf, Mr Aguilar. Your brother—' he looked to where Gael was swaying on the dance floor, smiling down at the woman in his arms '—he has his issues, but he has a better understanding of what the term *family* means. You, on the other hand, do not. My grandsons may very well override my wishes—they have the majority vote, after all. But I mean to sway them to my way of thinking.'

'Which is what exactly?' He was only mildly curious, the decision to walk away solidifying with each passing minute.

'That selling what I've spent my lifetime building to a man who is so determined to reject his blood and his past won't end well. Ishikawa Corporation is about family. I won't go to my grave without ensuring my legacy remains intact.'

'And that's your final word on the matter?' Alejandro asked.

'You'll do one of two things. You'll either walk away from this deal, or you'll reassess your priorities and do what is necessary for your own soul. Either way, I wish you the best. But I urge you to do the latter.'

The old man's parting words struck him hard. Alejandro sat, frozen in place, as Kenzo rose and shuffled off. He wasn't aware how long he sat there, staring at the water. It might have been three minutes. Or three hours.

But words he'd pushed away for a long time suddenly surged back, pounding through his brain.

Family. Compromise. Brother. Legacy.

When he sensed a presence behind him, Alejandro didn't need to look to know it was his brother. Gael took the seat Kenzo had vacated, his elbows braced on his knees. He looked as if he needed a drink.

'You met with the old man?'

Alejandro nodded.

'Did he give you the *family* spiel, too?'

'*Sí*, he did.'

Gael sighed. 'I guess you win this round. Kudos to you.'

Alejandro frowned. 'What?'

Gael spread his hands. 'I have to give it to you, it was a good move. Although, I thought…' He shook his head. 'Forget what I thought.'

'Gael, what are you talking about?'

His brother froze. 'I don't think I've ever heard you use my name.'

The pang in Alejandro's chest was deep and painful. 'Well. Perhaps…' He paused, not quite sure how to proceed. 'When this is done, we need to talk.'

Gael's smile was grim and unwelcoming. 'So I can listen to you gloat? No, thanks. Your neat trick paid off. You bagged this one. Accept the congrats and let's retreat to our respective kingdoms, *sí*?'

'I don't play tricks.' He spiked his fingers through his hair. 'Look, things didn't happen the way you thought they did…those three weeks when your mother went missing.'

Gael frowned. 'I was *there*, I know what happened.'

'You thought I was too busy chasing girls to help you. I wasn't. I was dealing with my own mother and the breakdown she was having over the whole thing.'

Gael's mouth twisted. 'Right.'

Alejandro sighed. 'You found her in the end, didn't you?'

'No thanks to you.'

Alejandro's smile felt as stiff and grim as his soul. 'You found her thanks to a note shoved under your door at half-past eight on a Saturday night. I can repeat the exact words on the note if you want?'

His brother's face went slack. *'You?'*

Alejandro nodded. 'The time when I wasn't trying to talk my mother down from full-blown depression, I was trying to get my father to come home. I attended soccer practice because my coach warned me he'd throw me off the team if I missed any more games.'

Gael shook his head. 'You…' he breathed again.

'It wasn't as easy for me as you think. Trust me on that.'

His brother stared at him for an age, before he nodded. 'Okay.'

Alejandro stared off at the reflective lake for a minute before he turned around. 'The deal is yours if you want it.'

Gael looked puzzled. 'Why would you hand me a deal that's already yours? I wouldn't have gone that way myself, but you played your ace and you won. There's no need to be coy about it.'

'*Santa Maria*, I have zero idea what you're talking about,' he growled.

'I'm talking about Elise.' Gael shook his head. 'Bringing an exquisitely beautiful woman with Japanese ancestry to pave the path for you? She's playing the part to perfection, I have to give her that. The old man is eating out of her hand. And if my eyesight is still twenty-twenty, Jason's set on getting lucky before the night is out.'

Cold dread tightened Alejandro's nape. He lunged for Gael's lapels. *What did you say?*

'I said—'

'Where is she?'

Gael drew back sharply. 'Hey—'

'Where?'

His brother pointed to the gardens at the side of the pavilion.

He barely felt the ground beneath his feet as he sprinted towards the cluster of cherry-blossom trees. The few guests who'd drifted out to enjoy the evening air hurried out of his way. His frenzied gaze darted over them, searching for her.

She wasn't there.

A quick three-sixty turn and he wondered whether Gael had got it wrong. But then he spotted an archway into another garden. The typical Japanese garden was designed around a pond of lotus flowers, water lilies and rock steps.

Alejandro appreciated none of that as he stepped over a short bridge and arrived at a shallow waterfall that fed the lake. To one side of it pooled a larger pond, with a love seat at the end of it, complete with mood lighting.

He froze at the sight before him, shock and disbelief colluding to tell him he was hallucinating. But then a more urgent sensation took hold. The ever-tightening vice around his heart forced him to breathe through the shock, to blink away the disbelief.

To acknowledge that Elise was indeed in Jason's arms.

Kissing him.

'Elise.' His voice was a ragged croak. She didn't hear him. Her eyes were shut, her face concentrated...hand on his chest...lost in the kiss.

His dead feet stumbled closer, every atom in his body hoping he'd mistaken her for someone else. But it was her. The red dress. The hair. The *body.*

'Dios mio. Elise!'

They parted unhurriedly, as if he were a nuisance they were reluctant to deal with.

Jason raised his head, speared him with a triumphant look. 'Mr Aguilar, you're intruding on a—'

'Do not speak!' he snarled, his gaze fixed on Elise's back, which remained rigidly turned to him. 'Turn around, Elise. *Now.'*

She turned slowly. Her face was coolly indifferent. But her eyes blinked sultrily as if she was drunk. *Drunk on another man's kiss.*

'Explain this to me,' he rasped.

One shoulder lifted. 'I would've thought it was obvious?'

The loud clanging in his head wouldn't stop. *'Why?'*

'I don't owe you any explanations, Alejandro. Not when it comes to my personal life. Just as you don't owe me any about yours.'

Alejandro stared at her, heard the cool words. Still his mind refused to compute.

'Was there something else you needed?'

Shaky fingers spiked his hair. '*Madre de Dios*, I thought you were *different*.'

An expression crossed her face, but he was too far gone to read it accurately. But then her features settled once more into serene, *treacherous* perfection. 'I *am* different, Alejandro. Shame you're too blind to see it.'

CHAPTER ELEVEN

Six months later

ALEJANDRO STARED AT his flashing phone. Margo wouldn't put the call through if it weren't essential. She'd borne the consequence of not heeding his *do not disturb* edict the single time she'd taken her eye off that particular ball.

A fleeting twinge in some remote corner of his being was the only sign that he regretted his scathing reaction to her mishap. To her credit, she hadn't cried. Or thrown a tantrum. She'd sucked it up and made sure it didn't happen again.

He admired that. Her ability to be what he wanted her to be. If he was brutally honest with himself, Margo was the only constant in his life.

Now that everything had changed.

Which made him certain this call was probably important.

He started to reach for it. It stopped ringing. He exhaled in relief and turned in his seat. About to rise and head to his window, he paused as his mobile began to ring.

He recognised Gael's number. This twinge was a different sort. A hint of apprehension. Anticipation. His brother had called only once since Japan. The conversation had been tense, the past tentatively broached. It had by no means been a reconciliatory call, and Alejandro wasn't certain if they'd ever get there.

But somewhere in his heart a tiny sprouting of hope lingered. He hadn't decided whether to feed it yet...

He picked up the phone and slid his thumb across the surface. 'Alejandro.'

'Good to know you're alive. Now I don't have to badger your PA into listening at your door for signs of life,' Gael drawled.

'Anything in particular I can help you with?' he demanded gruffly.

Gael paused a tense beat. 'Your diary is clear for the next two hours. And no, Margo didn't divulge that information. I graduated first in my class from MIT. I know my way around computer code.'

Alejandro gritted his teeth. 'Please tell me you did not just admit to hacking my company's system?'

'Of course not. Your appointment is with me.'

Discomfort moved through him, but then so did

a certain level of acceptance. For better or worse, Gael was his brother. The question now remained how to move forward with this. 'Then why are you calling me beforehand?'

'You have a private chef. I'm proposing a lunch meeting to discuss new developments.'

Alejandro exhaled. 'The food will be taken care of. Explain the second part.'

Gael paused for a moment. 'The Ishikawa deal may be back on the table.'

'I'm not interested.'

His brother made an impatient sound. 'I'll be there in ten. We'll discuss this further.' He hung up before Alejandro could draw breath.

After relaying instructions to Margo, he tossed the phone down and jerked to his feet. He started to head for his window, but changed course at the last moment.

This was something else she'd ruined. He couldn't enjoy the view now without remembering her sketch of him standing at this very window, staring out. She'd seen inside him. Uncovered what he'd spent over a decade trying to hide.

She'd made him believe there was a connection between them.

But it'd been a lie.

She'd changed everything.

His world had been an acceptable regiment of clinical routine before her. SNV was his number one priority. Nothing else mattered.

Elise Jameson had thrown a grenade into that existence. She'd made him feel. Worse, she'd made him…*hope.* To think he'd actually been considering making adjustments in his life that included family and compromise. That he'd spent that hour in Kenzo's garden, seeking ways to accommodate the new and uncharted into his life.

When all the while she'd been pursuing another agenda. So far he'd stopped himself from dissecting which part of her history had been a lie. Her claimed innocence? The fact that landing one of the Ishikawa brothers had been an addendum to her job or her goal from the beginning, probably orchestrated by her grandmother? Because when Alejandro thought about it, he noticed that she'd resisted any discussion about *them.* Any pursuit of a sexual nature had come from Alejandro. Because she hadn't been interested?

No. She had been. He wasn't insane enough to have misread their chemistry.

But she still fell into another man's arms.

Balling his fists, he shoved them into his pockets and turned his back on the view, just as the door opened and his brother entered.

Gael was dressed for an early start to the weekend, if his jeans, T-shirt and leather biker jacket were any indication. The mid-October temperatures were balmy enough not to require further covering, which suited his west coast resident brother.

They exchanged a less stiff nod, then Gael crossed to the drinks cabinet and pour two cognacs. He handed one to Alejandro.

'You don't think this is premature? Celebrating a dead deal before a conversation has even taken place?'

Gael shrugged as he sat down on the sofa, his focus slightly pensive. 'Prematurity means there's something to *mature* into.'

Alejandro downed the drink, revelling for a single mindless moment in the warmth that flowed through him because he knew it wouldn't last. 'You're pushy.'

'I'm relentless. And ruthless.' Gael sipped his drink. 'And you're the man I keep hearing all these formidable stories about. From this side of the room, I'm not seeing much evidence of it,' he mocked.

'You flew all the way here from California with this feeble tactic? To reverse-psych me into entering into this deal with you?'

Gael raised a brow. 'Tell me if it's working and I'll tailor my answer accordingly.'

'It's not working.'

The knock on the door halted a response. Margo entered. 'Your food is ready. Shall I set it up in here or the dining room?'

Alejandro pried himself from the wall. 'In here. And take the rest of the afternoon off, Margo.'

Her eyes widened. 'Really?'

He nodded. 'Enjoy your weekend.'

The food was delivered. Gael devoured half of the club sandwich before he sat back and wiped his mouth on a napkin. Alejandro lost his appetite after one bite.

'The Ishikawas are prepared to go forward with the merger. With *both* of us.'

Alejandro opened his mouth to dismiss the offer outright, but paused. 'Why?'

'Why not? It's the best of all worlds. You bring the e-commerce arm, I deliver the digital streaming and cloud-based services. They provide the infrastructure. Together we'll be unstoppable.'

Just as Elise had suggested.

He watched Gael pick up his remaining sandwich and bite into it, and tried to swallow past the ashes in his own mouth.

Pushing his plate away, he shook his head. 'There

are no guarantees they won't start getting us to jump through hoops again. It doesn't work for me.'

Gael's unforgiving gaze connected with his. 'Is that the real reason? Or it is something—or someone—else? Someone like Elise, perhaps?'

He froze. 'Watch it,' he warned.

Of course, his brother didn't heed him. 'Six months later and you're still hung up about her?'

'Suficiente!'

Gael plucked a bottle of water off the table and gulped down several mouthfuls. 'Have you seen her since Kyoto?'

Alejandro's insides knotted. Icy fury and other emotions he didn't want to name wrestled within him. 'No. Why are you asking me this?'

'Because you're right. There's one tiny condition to this deal.'

A hot curse erupted from him before he could stop it. 'I'm overwhelmed with shock.'

Gael grimaced. 'The old man wants Elise back in on the deal.'

'Ni hablar! Hell, no.'

Gael's jaw clenched. 'We're both businessmen, Andro. There have been women in the past and there will be women in the future—hey, don't growl at me. If you intend to live like a monk, go right ahead. But you're letting her get in the way of a revolutionary deal. The longest she'll need to be involved in the negotiations is a couple of months. Are you telling me you can't handle that?'

'Don't test me, Gael,' he snarled, deeply unsettled by the raw sensations moving inside him.

His brother eyed him for a minute, then reached into his pocket. 'Your private life is your own. But this is business.' He pulled out a folded piece of paper and set it down on the table. 'You'll need this if you want the deal to go ahead. When you decide, call me.' Gael walked to the door. 'Thanks for lunch,' he tossed over his shoulder before he exited.

Alejandro stared at the paper for a full minute before he reached for it. The address was out of state. In fact it was several states away. But it wasn't the other side of the world. *It isn't Kyoto.*

The distant thrumming of his blood gathered speed. Grew louder.

The image of her in another man's arms tore through him. He'd walked away. He needed to let this be.

But…

I am different… Shame you're too blind to see it.

She'd dared to taunt him. And in the last six months, those words had flashed through his mind more times than he cared for.

I am different…

He stared at the address until the letters were burned into his retinas.

It looked as if he was going to Montana.

The sound of the vehicle thundering down the dirt road was different from the rattle of tractors or Steven's banged-up old truck. Elise was in the zone, so she didn't lift her head or move an inch from her position beneath the apple tree. She continued to sketch, sending a silent plea that her rare moment of concentration wouldn't be disturbed.

Peace had been so hard to come by. Ironically, the more breathtaking the landscape in Montana grew, the unhappier she became. Summer had been the worst. Sultry evenings that were handpicked for harvest and lovers had seen her curled up in bed, stifling her sobs with her fist. In those desolate weeks, she'd wished for the numbness of May and June, when her emotions had remained in suspended animation. Because with the thaw had come the stark truth that her feelings for Alejandro were in no way resolved. Another truth was knowing the way she'd handled that last night in Kyoto had hammered nails into a door she wished she could prise open just one last time.

The thaw had exposed the depth of her craving for him; how deep the hurt and pain that resided in her heart ran. It'd also reminded her why she'd had to end any hope of a connection with Alejandro.

There's no heart there to sustain meaningful relationships.

Elise hadn't known a handful of words could turn her world black until she'd heard them.

Then she'd known.

She'd been fooling herself by contemplating a dalliance with Alejandro. So she'd drawn a definite line through any possibility. She'd needed to, to preserve her own heart.

Except her heart had gone and broken all the same. On top of that, he'd taken her creativity away again. For four long months, she'd been unable to pick up her pencil. Even drawing him had been too much when all she could recall was his face that last time she'd seen him.

The urge to abandon her dream again had been strong, but the thought of losing both Alejandro *and* her art had been unbearable, so she'd soldiered on.

The first attempts had been shockingly abysmal. But she'd persisted, dredged pockets of time when Alejandro hadn't been dominating her thoughts. Pockets where she'd dreamed he was standing before her, a hint of a smile on his face even as those mesmeric eyes bore into her—

'Elise.'

Her head jerked up. The pencil dropped from her numb fingers. Vital air strangled in her lungs as she blinked hard, sure he was an apparition.

'Alejandro?'

He crested the hill and towered over her, his eyes inscrutable as he stared down at her.

'What—' She stopped, looked around. Nothing gave her a clue, so she attempted again. 'What are you doing here?'

His mouth firmed in a painfully familiar show of displeasure. 'Hunting you down, of course. What else?' His tone implied he wouldn't otherwise be caught dead in the rolling mountains of the midwest.

'And why would you want to do that?' she queried, her heart still attempting to jackhammer out of her chest. To give herself something to do besides stare with fervid attention at his enthralling face, his hard-packed—albeit leaner—body, she started gathering up her art supplies.

'We have unfinished business.'

A gasp attempted to form. It died in her throat. 'No. I'm sure we don't.' That last night in Kyoto had been definitive in every way. The reminder was effective in reducing her pulse from light speed to mere jet propelled.

She stood, zipped up her sketch case and fiercely

resisted the urge to smooth her unruly hair. She'd let it grow in the last six months, her inclination to groom it, or herself, non-existent. The result was a wavy mess that hung halfway down her back, framing the denim shorts and a seriously unsexy plain T-shirt she'd picked up on one of her rare trips into Portland.

When his silence thickened, she risked a glance at Alejandro. To find his rapier-sharp gaze scouring her from head to toe.

'You've lost weight.'

'You didn't come all this way to tell me that, I'm sure.' She started down the hill.

He caught her arm. 'We need to talk, Elise.'

'I can't imagine what you'd want to talk to me about.' She tried to pull away. Admittedly she didn't put much effort into it because the tingling warmth seeping into her felt embarrassingly good.

Alejandro's hold firmed nevertheless. 'The man I met down there. Who is he?' he scythed at her.

'Steven? He owns the ranch.'

'And?'

'And nothing.'

His nostrils flared. 'Elise.'

She tugged harder. He released her, but prowled closer when she stepped back. 'What gives you the right to come here and question me? We said all we had to say in Kyoto, remember? Our business is over and done with.'

Arctic green eyes snapped at her. 'Not quite.'

Dread found a foothold inside her. 'What are you talking about? You terminated the contract with Jameson. I saw the paperwork.'

'I *suspended* it because I had no interim work to make up for the unfinished commission, but I paid the full commission your parents demanded.'

Cold disbelief engulfed her. 'You can't possibly want me back. What do you need me for that your PR department can't handle?'

Emotion flicked in his eyes, but the slant of the mid-afternoon sun made it difficult for her to read it accurately. 'The Ishikawa deal is back on. Kenzo insists you be part of my team.'

Her heart lurched. Squashing the despondency that came from knowing Alejandro was truly only here for business, she shook her head. 'I can't just… leave.'

His face tightened. 'Why not?'

'Because I have responsibilities. Jobs I have to do around the ranch in order to pay my way.'

He frowned. 'You left Chicago to mess around with cows and horses? What about your art? Or pursuing your dream?'

Elise took a few more steps away from him, as

if that would stop the probing questions. 'I'm not playing twenty questions with you, Alejandro. Especially about my personal life. What I would like to do is to work something out with you about how to pay off the rest of the commission—'

'You can pay it off by coming back to finish what you started. I'm afraid it's non-negotiable.'

She raised her head then, stared into his beautiful, implacable face. The thought of going back to work in close proximity with Alejandro, suffering his presence while knowing that there would never be a future for them together, slayed her. She couldn't do it.

'I can't.'

Restless energy charged from him. '*Sí*, you can. You speak about responsibilities and obligations. You have a responsibility to finish what you started with SNV.'

'Or what?' she flung at him, desperation fuelling the brazen demand.

He stared down at her for a handful of seconds, before he shook his head. 'I won't threaten you, Elise.' His voice was low, a little ragged around the edges. 'You showed me your true colours in Kyoto. So I'll leave it entirely up to you as to whether you want to do the right thing or not.'

If only he'd threatened. Or tried to blackmail her.

She would've stood a chance. But Alejandro hadn't achieved global success without knowing which buttons to press to achieve the results he wanted. And by striking at the heart of her integrity, he'd left her with nothing to fight back.

'So is that a yes?' he pressed. He'd moved closer. Enough for her to feel his body heat. She locked her knees to prevent herself from closing the gap between them, inhaling the scent she hadn't realised all those months ago that she would miss until it was gone.

'That depends.'

'On what?'

'On how long until you expect this merger to be finalised.'

His eyes narrowed. 'What's the hurry?'

'I have a life to get on with. I may be contractually obligated to finish what I started with you, but that doesn't mean I'm content to put my life on hold indefinitely.'

His mouth compressed. In the distance, a tractor droned on. 'Are you in such a hurry to get back here? To your lazy afternoons under the apple tree?' he sneered.

'If that's your roundabout way of asking if I miss the cut-throat world of high finance, then no, I don't miss it. I miss *nothing* at all about Chicago.'

Ripples of emotions ghosted over his face, and had she wanted to fool herself, she'd have imagined her words had wounded him somehow. But she was too busy convincing herself of the lies she told her heart to fathom his feelings.

Besides, she needed to remember that the only reason he was here was because of his precious merger. 'How long, Alejandro?' she asked briskly.

'One month. Six weeks at the most, to accommodate visits to the countries we settle on for the initial satellite bases of operation. Is that agreeable to you?' he asked.

Six weeks to draw a definite line under her association with Alejandro. To train her heart to live without him all over again.

She swallowed past the rock of anguish lodged in her midriff, and, with a single jerk of her head, sealed her fate. 'Yes.'

He took the case and waited, silent and powerful as she gathered the small picnic basket and blanket, then escorted her down the hill to the ranch house.

When she saw the sleek SUV parked in front of the ranch house, her heart jumped into her throat. 'When do you need me to come to Chicago? I'll look into flights tonight and email you tomorrow...'

She trailed off as he shook his head. 'I didn't come all this way to return without you, Elise.

You'll pack what you need and we'll take my plane back tonight.'

She didn't see the point in arguing. Apart from the fruitlessness of it, going back with Alejandro would mean she wouldn't have to raid her meagre savings to pay for her flight.

Handing in her notice and turning her back on Jameson PR had been freeing, but it'd also left her without an income.

As for her parents, they had tried to guilt her into staying. There'd been accusations revolving around the loss of the SNV contract, but Elise had been too steeped in the fog of pain to pay them much attention. Her debt to her parents was paid. Her father had made a half-hearted attempt to stay in touch during her first weeks in Montana. Her mother had emailed.

Elise had answered dutifully, but her heart had been too heavy to make much of an attempt. It still was. But she'd accepted that the only way her parents would truly embrace her was if she shared their dreams. It hurt to know that would never happen, but she would learn to live with it.

Steven stepped out onto the porch. He nodded at her, then his gaze swung to Alejandro.

Her old college friend's offer of room and board in return for odd jobs around his ranch had saved

Elise six months ago. Steven Bosworth had for the most part let her be, content to share the odd beer with her on his porch when his busy day was done.

She'd seen the concerned looks he'd sent her when he thought she wasn't aware, but thankfully he hadn't pushed her.

'Steven, this is—'

'There's no need to introduce us. We've already met,' Alejandro inserted, his voice tight.

'Everything all right, Elise?' Steven asked.

'Yes, I'm just—'

'I'm on a tight schedule, Elise. You have five minutes to pack,' Alejandro said, his deep voice thick with formidable authority.

'You're being rude. And I'll be more than five minutes. If you're in that much of a hurry, leave without me. I'll catch the next available flight,' Elise said firmly.

Eyes the colour of frozen moss glared at her. She glared right back, but, in some corner of her being, excitement leaped. She'd never thought she'd ever cross paths with Alejandro again, never mind lock horns with him. Now that she was, she wanted to argue with him for ever.

The thought was frightening enough to propel her back a step.

He shadowed her move. 'Ten minutes, Elise.'

'Twenty, *Alejandro*.'

He didn't respond, only made the short trip to his SUV, her sketch case still in his hand. Pressing on a fob, he tossed the case into the back and slammed the boot.

Returning to the front of the vehicle, he leaned against the bumper, arms crossed, eyes laser-fixed on her. 'You have nineteen minutes, and counting. One second over that and I'll drag you out.'

The sound she made was unladylike. Turning, she startled, having forgotten Steven's silent witnessing of their exchange from the porch. Heat rushed up her face as she grimaced.

'I guess from all that…*spiky* conversation that you're leaving?' he murmured.

She nodded as she climbed the porch. 'I'm sorry, Steven. I don't really have a choice.'

His eyes narrowed, but she waved him away. 'It's not as grim as that. I just have…unfinished business to attend to,' she said, repeating Alejandro's words.

'Okay. Will you be back?' he asked.

About to answer in the affirmative, Elise stopped. 'I don't know,' she murmured. Steven's ranch had been a much-needed sanctuary, but she couldn't hide out here for ever. Once Alejandro was well and truly behind her, it would be time to forge the path she'd always dreamed of.

She swallowed past the ragged pain still lodged in her midriff, and smiled at Steven. 'I'll let you know in a day or two, okay?'

He nodded, his sand-coloured hair gleaming gold in the late afternoon sun. 'You have a standing invitation to stay any time you want. Least I can do to repay you for the free PR and advice on how to get the stud farm up and running.' His glance slid past her to a bristling Alejandro. 'You better hop to it before something catches fire around here.'

She glanced over at Alejandro. His jaw was locked. His eyes mere slits as he observed them. Sucking in a breath, she darted into the century-old two-storey ranch house Steven had inherited along with the farm. Her room was at the top of the stairs.

As she packed her meagre belongings into the single suitcase, she accepted that her stay here had only ever been a stop-gap. She'd been marking time until she could come alive again.

But while she felt alive now, her heart dipped with wrenching anguish to also accept that in a few short weeks she would need to continue feeling alive, without Alejandro.

The man in question was stalking the porch when she opened the front door. And he kept right on coming. Once he had possession of her suitcase, he caught her arm and started to lead her away.

'Wait.' She ignored his growl, and crossed over to Steven, giving him a quick hug. 'Thanks for everything.'

'No problem. Seriously. Now go before he tears me limb from limb,' Steven muttered.

She went, her heart racing as she slid into the seat beside Alejandro. His exit from the ranch was aggressively fast and dusty. Hanging on, Elise fought the urge to roll her eyes. And failed.

'If I lived in an alternate universe, I'd say you were jealous.'

The SUV swerved to the side of the deserted road and screeched to a stop. Tension mounted until she was sure she could reach out and touch it. For the longest time, he stared at her and just breathed; heavy, chest-filling breaths that vibrated right through her.

'For the sake of my ability to function, Elise, tell me you haven't spent the last six months in his bed?'

Her mouth dropped open. Her body flushed with heat. Then cold. 'I… Why on earth should that matter to you?'

A harsh laugh wrenched through the vehicle. 'Because contrary to the laws of common sense and everything that should dictate otherwise, you continue to rage like a damn *fever* in my blood.' The delivery was intense. A lethal blade cutting through everything he'd said in the last hour. Striking the heart of his presence here. 'I want you. I crave you. Despite everything.'

Her low gasp dissolved before it'd even fully emerged. '*Despite* everything? You hate yourself for feeling the way you do about me, don't you?'

Another ragged exhalation. 'A lot of things have ceased to make sense to me. *Including* this.'

While she was trying to compute that, he lunged for her, buried his fingers in her loose hair and gripped her tight. '*Por el amor de Dios*, tell me!'

'Why should I?' she hissed, anger and hurt scything through her despite the intoxicating proximity of him. When his breath feathered hot and decadent over her mouth, she almost lost her ability to think. 'There's nothing between you and I, Alejandro.'

His nostrils flared with towering rage, before he let out a harsh laugh. 'You made sure of that by falling into another man's arms!' he charged with a quiet fury that was no less volcanic for its rumble.

She pulled away, at once afraid of the depth of her feelings and the temptation of him. 'I was—'

'*Dios mio*, you were kissing another man, when I couldn't have made it clearer that I wanted you to be mine!' One hand spiked through his hair before it balled into a fist.

'Yes, *you* wanted! Did you ever stop to think about what *I* wanted?'

His features tautened. 'What are you talking about? Nothing excuses what I saw.'

'In that case why are we having this conversation?'

He seethed for tense seconds.

'Because I can't get you out of my head.'

The words were stark. Rough. Jagged.

Her heart lurched as they stared at each other across the console. 'Tell me you've gotten me out of yours.'

She shook her head, the words clogging her throat.

'I want to hear the words, Elise,' he stressed.

Her mouth parted, ready to issue lies. But they locked, strangled, morphed into other words. Words that she knew before she uttered them would doom her. She'd wished for the door she'd slammed shut to open one more time. She was getting her chance. 'I haven't been able to get you out of mine,' she murmured.

Alejandro's eyes glinted with a mixture of satisfaction and disillusionment, as if he'd found a prize that had turned out to be only semi-precious.

He threw the car into gear and accelerated down the dirt road.

She cleared her throat. 'Alejandro, I need to explain what happened with Jason—'

'No,' he cut in coldly. 'I don't wish to hear it. You've told me the only thing that matters. It may be six months longer than I anticipated, but I'll have you in my bed, Elise. You'll come to me. You will enjoy it. And when we're done, we'll walk away from each other. But I never want to hear you utter his name again. Is that clear?'

CHAPTER TWELVE

SHE WAS IN deep trouble. Elise had thought she'd sorted through her feelings in the six months Alejandro had been out of her life, but she found out very quickly that being around him was tantamount to living in emotional chaos. And a determined Alejandro only made things worse.

The first exhibition of the juggernaut that was Alejandro's sheer willpower came her way even before she'd stepped on his plane. The second she responded 'no' to having a place to stay, he nodded.

'We don't have time to find you an apartment. You'll stay with me.'

He'd taken the same dominating path to his discovery that her one suitcase only contained clothes fit for ranch work and work boots. Clothes had arrived in her suite in his multimillion-dollar penthouse displaying designer labels that made her gasp. Her hasty, 'I can't accept these!' had been met with an inflexible, 'You can and you will. If it eases your sensibilities, donate them to charity when you're done with them.'

Of course, the reminder that their time together was finite had robbed her of breath and an adequate response. She'd fallen back into the routine of being his eyes and ears. Only this time, Alejandro demanded her stronger participation with client liaisons; had taken to touching her hand or arm to gain her attention when her focus strayed for even a second; his trips into her small office were more frequent, and his gaze lingered long and hungrily on her body when they were alone. Most evenings they dined out, although conversation during their meals was stilted, with Alejandro barely eating more than a few mouthfuls while she wasn't allowed to leave a meal unfinished.

But there'd been no kisses, no attempt to take her to bed.

And more than once, she'd encountered his harsh, disillusioned stare that dragged icicles across her heart.

As she slipped her feet into four-inch heels and smoothed her hands down her black pinstriped dress in readiness to join Alejandro for breakfast before they headed in to work, her heart squeezed painfully, even as she admitted the wait was driving her slowly insane.

It had disturbed more than a few nights' sleep, which had in turn fuelled a frenzy of sketches. It hadn't surprised her when she'd noted that all the stories charted a tale of heartache and loss.

Pushing the state of her turbulent emotions aside, she caught up the matching jacket and her handbag and left her bedroom.

The scent of freshly ground coffee drew her to the dining room, and she smiled as she passed Alejandro's butler, Sergio.

'Buenos días, querida,' Alejandro drawled, his hard gaze skimming over her before returning to the paper in his hand.

Breathing through her escalated heartbeat, she returned the greeting, sat down and helped herself to a cream-cheese-spread bagel and coffee.

'Anything of interest in the paper?' she asked.

'Surprisingly, not even a whisper,' he replied, a hard smile doing nothing to soften his sculptured features.

Speculation had been rife for the past week, with financial pundits going wild with what the rumours of the SNV/Ishikawa/Toredo deal would mean if it went ahead.

Alejandro's in-house PR department, with her supervisory input, had kept a tight leash on all press releases. But by day's end, the Aguilar brothers would make history.

Because today, two weeks after dragging her

back to Chicago, Alejandro and Gael would final-
ise the merger.

Her blood thrummed in anticipation of what tonight would bring, her excitement unable to be suppressed despite the quiet pride and awe she felt
in being part of this financial-landscape-changing
merger.

'Are you ready for the ride?' he asked.

Despite the casual nature of the question, there
was an edge to his voice, one that made her hackles rise.

She knew what he was asking.

She'd sensed that Alejandro was waiting for
the merger to be signed before making his move.
Whereas she'd been ready to take the insane leap
back on that dirt road in Montana.

She raised her head and locked eyes with his narrowed ones. 'Yes.'

He nodded once, stood and held out his hand. She
slipped her hand into his and he pulled her up. His
gaze dropped to her lips.

Unbearable need propelled her tongue into a
quick swipe of her lower lip.

Alejandro made a rough sound in his throat, his
eyes losing focus for a second. Then he stepped
back, and straightened his faultless tie.

The ride to The Loop was fast, his Bugatti eating

up the miles. Elise walked at his side as they entered his building, the tension between them growing thicker with each second.

At SNV the mood was one of muted excitement. Gael's presence took a little bit of Alejandro's focus off her, but all through the excitement-tinged day she sensed his gaze tracking her, the ominous intensity leaving her in no doubt that, one way or the other, the subject of their own personal merger was about to be broached.

Kenzo Ishikawa arrived with his grandsons at two. By three o'clock the documents were signed. Alejandro gathered his employees in the largest conference room and broke the news to thunderous applause, then stood beside Gael as he did the same via video link with his employees in California.

After champagne toasts were given, the entourage headed to the ground floor where the press had gathered.

Elise spotted her parents the moment she stepped out of the lift. They were holding court with the rest of SNV's PR team in preparation to head into the conference.

They'd tried to inveigle their way, via her, into getting more commissions from SNV. When Elise had made it painfully clear she was only back to finish the work she'd started, they'd requested in-clusion into the press conferences scheduled for when the merger was formally announced.

Her mother sent a dismissive glance that made her stiffen with hurt.

Alejandro glanced sharply at her. 'What's wrong?'

'Nothing I want to ruin your day with.'

His eyes narrowed. Then he scoured the room until he spotted her parents. 'If I'd known they would cause you this much distress, I would've had their invitation revoked.'

She shook her head. 'No. I'm serious. Don't con-cern yourself about this.'

'You need to remind yourself that falling in with them would've been so much easier than resisting. You chose a different path. A better path.' His hand lightly holding her wrist tightened, imbuing her with warmth. 'Give yourself credit for that at least.'

The unexpected accolade hit her square in the chest. Her breath shook as her eyes met his. 'Okay... I... umm, thanks.'

He gave a curt nod.

Gael approached, his own tension adding to the almost capricious excitement. 'We ready to do this?' he rasped.

Alejandro's glance lingered on her, his expres-sion taut. '*Sí*. I'm ready.'

* * *

Four hours later, Elise stood in front of her mirror. This time her attire was far removed from office chic. The dinner party Alejandro had decided to host to celebrate the merger would start in fifteen minutes.

She'd opted for a 1920s-style cocktail dress in a deep green with a sequin-fringed hem and capped sleeves. The heavy chiffon skimmed her curves and ended a few inches above her knee. But while she loved the style, she was ashamed to admit that she'd chosen the colour because it matched Alejandro's eyes.

She drew a brush through her hair, her movements slowing as she recalled his words to her this afternoon. Her heart performed a worryingly familiar somersault, even though her more feet-on-the-ground mind told her she risked a whole lot more than a dizzy spell if she read more into Alejandro's words than the blatantly carnal.

But she couldn't deny his words had provided a much-needed balm. She'd been able to withstand her parents' preening and brazen spotlight seeking without feeling the urge to retreat into her own world. And her mother's narrow-eyed assessment of her dress and smug conclusion that Elise was finally taking her advice and getting what she could from her relationship with Alejandro had bounced off her for the first time in her life.

A knock on her door drew her from her musings. Alejandro stood tall and proud in her doorway, his customary black shirt and charcoal suit swapped for a black dinner jacket and snowy white shirt.

Dizzyingly overwhelmed by his presence, she stepped back. 'I'm just about—'

'*Dios mio*, you look breathtaking.'

Her blush should've embarrassed her. She should've wrung her hands and sought self-deprecating words. But something earthy and powerful in his eyes made her chin rise, her spine straightening as she drank in his compliment, for the first time, accepting and acknowledging her femininity without bitterness or shame.

'*Muchas gracias.*' She murmured the words she'd heard him use.

His eyes darkened and her pleasure escalated.

They stood like that, staring. Appreciating. Acknowledging *their* impending merger. And even when the trace of cynicism crossed his eyes, her excitement didn't dim.

He reached into his jacket pocket. 'I have something for you.'

'I... What?'

'A gift to remind you of a momentous day.' He held out the box.

'There's no risk that I'll forget it any time soon. You don't need to give me a gift.'

'I'm doing it all the same.'

'Alejandro—'

'We're arguing again,' he murmured, his jaw slightly clenched.

'You like our arguments.' She attempted to lighten the mood, unable to drag her eyes from the olive-skinned beauty of him, or her senses from the intoxicating scent of him.

'I do. They drive me half insane, but the victory is always worth it.'

Her eyes widened. 'The victory?'

'*Sí*, you always inevitably capitulate, but not before you make me jump through hoops.'

'I *don't…*' She stopped, her mind drifting back to realise that it was true. Somehow Alejandro got his way in the end.

'Take the gift, *querida*. My arm is about to fall off from the strain.'

She took it, partly out of curiosity and partly because she was still replaying his words. Reason took flight as she opened the box and saw the glittering gems.

'Alejandro! I can't take this. It's not... What would your team think?' she blurted.

'They'll think themselves incredibly lucky to be working for me since they all received bonuses of their own.'

'Oh...' The diamond bracelet was exquisite, the design simple but flawless.

He took the bracelet from its velvet bed and secured it around her wrist. Then taking her hand, he kissed the back of it. Elise didn't miss the hard triumphant light in his eyes as he placed her hand in the crook of his arm.

Mild dread shivered down her spine, but she pushed it away, attempting to lighten the tension once again. 'No need to look so smug.'

His mouth twitched in a tight smile. 'There's every need, *mi corazón*. I have you exactly where I want you.'

Alejandro kept ahold of her all through the party. And even though they drew more than a few speculative glances, Elise didn't care. Her decision was made and cemented in her heart. Besides, although it hadn't happened yet, Alejandro's constant attention in the form of little touches had already sparked enough rumours to snowball its own story.

She went with the flow, chatted to acquaintances

and executives from all three companies, with the exception of Jason Ishikawa, whose name had been blatantly excluded from the guest list.

She was walking away from Jason's brother, Nathan, when a hand slid around her waist. 'You were right about one thing,' Alejandro drawled in her ear.

Her smile wasn't as full as she hoped. 'Just the one?' she teased.

She expected a quick comeback, and her steps faltered when he didn't answer immediately. Stopping in the hollowed-out space between reception rooms, she faced him, her heart thudding sickeningly.

'Alejandro…I think we need to talk. Clear the air?'

His mouth tightened. The look on his face was harsh. And yet vulnerable. Elise was stabbed with the visceral urge to comfort him, but she remained still.

'I'm not sure what *talking* will achieve, *querida*. And *sí*, you were right. I'm jealous of every man who looks at you. Of every man you smile at,' he breathed.

Her soft gasp landed between them. 'It's…I…'

'It's irrational. And deplorable, considering I know how detrimental such feelings can be.' His gaze flicked to hers as if he was gauging her reaction.

Elise gave in to her need and cupped his cheek. 'It's only deplorable if you deliberately use it to hurt or manipulate. As for the rationality of it...' She shrugged. 'Nathan Ishikawa's date was almost introduced to my irrational side when she flashed her cleavage at you for the third time at dinner. But I guess we all have our crosses to bear, don't we?'

One corner of his mouth lifted. The harshness dissipated. He laid his hand over hers and pressed her back until her shoulders touched the wall. His gaze scoured her face with an intensity that bordered on fanatic, before locking on her mouth. 'Smile for me, Elise *mio*. Just for me,' he ordered thickly.

Her breath shook out, and her mouth wobbled with her first attempt. But her smile shone through and stayed when she heard his strangled groan.

'You look nothing like her,' he mused roughly.

Elise tensed. 'Like who?'

'A painting that briefly hung in my father's study. The first time I saw you, you reminded me of that painting. But I see now it's only a passing resemblance. Your smile, your face, is so much more exceptional.'

Some of the tension seeped out of her. 'Was that why you reacted to me the way you did?'

He inclined his head. 'Yes. I was captivated. I still am.'

She blushed. To cover her embarrassment, she blurted, 'Tell me more about the painting.'

His face shadowed. 'Regrettably, as with all things my father paid attention to, it caused too much friction for it to last. But there is one detail I recall though.'

'Yes?'

Dark hunger scorched her. 'She was nude.'

Her gasp was swallowed, her hand caught in his and curled against his chest as he kissed her, deep and long and masterfully. Elise moaned, strained closer until his hard body was imprinted against hers. The sound of clinking glasses and drifting voices finally made them part.

Alejandro's face was stamped with the same naked hunger clawing through her.

'I have waited long enough, *querida*. Tonight you'll be mine,' he commanded thickly. 'Say the words, Elise.'

Her heart lurched, then sped up its beat. 'I'll be yours,' she whispered.

His breath shuddered out. Cradling her hands between his, he kissed her knuckles, then drew her out of the alcove. Wordlessly, he led her back to the party.

Elise spent the rest of the evening drifting in a haze of anticipation and trepidation.

She'd pledged her virginity to a powerful, virile man who knew his way around a female body, whereas the circumstances of her upbringing had made her shy away from even the mention of sex. She knew the technicalities of the act, but beyond that she would be operating blind.

A hysterical bubble rose in her throat. Quickly swallowing it down, she tried to breathe through her nerves. She was still battling her way through her anxiety when Gael approached where she stood with Alejandro saying goodbye to the first wave of departing guests.

The brothers shook hands, a look passing between them that was almost too intense to witness. 'Not bad for a good day's work, huh?' Gael joked, but his eyes shone with more than just triumph. They shone with pride, and yearning for acceptance, both of which Alejandro's lopsided smile reflected.

'You have my permission to pat yourself on the back now.'

Gael snorted. 'That's what the girlfriends are for.' His expression veiled for a moment, then returned to Alejandro. 'I'm heading to Spain in the morning. I'll be back in time to join you for the first site tours at the end of the week.'

Alejandro had stiffened at the mention of his homeland. Imagining the subject disturbing enough to be dropped, she was surprised when he nodded. 'Do you see her often? Your mother?'

Eyes a few shades lighter than his shadowed before Gael's expression cleared. Shrugging, he said, 'She visits me in California a couple of times a year. I've set her up in a villa outside Barcelona. I try to see her when I can.'

Mild shock lit Alejandro's eyes. 'She's no longer in Seville?'

Gael shook his head. 'She moved ten years ago.' He paused a beat. 'Reconnecting should be easier now…for all concerned.'

Alejandro's tension mounted. 'The past needs to stay where it belongs.'

His younger brother looked as if he wanted to debate the point, but eventually, he shrugged. *'Muy bien. Hasta luego, mi hermano.'*

This time their goodbye involved clasped hands and half-hugs.

Alejandro remained the attentive host to his remaining guests, but he got more brooding the later the evening grew. It didn't take a genius to guess Gael's words had penetrated to a vulnerable place. But the moment the last guest left, he strode across the living-room floor and seized Elise in his arms.

The kiss was ferocious, his need a living beast intent on devouring her. She met him in hunger and desire, her need just as potent. When hands framed her face, and his kiss deepened, something incredibly powerful jolted within her. She wanted to hang the sexual desire term on it, but Elise knew it was more. So much more.

For good or ill—and a dark painful place within her suspected it might be the latter—she had fallen in love with Alejandro Aguilar. Deeply, irrevocably in love.

The beauty, purity and hauntingly doomed nature of her feeling caused tears to prickle her eyes. Desperate to seek the pleasure and forget the impending pain, she tightened her grip in his hair, luxuriating in the brilliant vitality of him.

He swung her into his arms without breaking the kiss. She didn't need to know where he was taking her. Surrender was as inevitable as breathing.

In his room, he placed her on her feet and broke the kiss. Eyes turned a dark, gleaming moss, fired only by hunger, unrelenting and all-encompassing, blazed down at her. His hands found the side zip of her dress, and tugged. The heavy material dropped, leaving her in the new white lingerie set she'd let the stylist talk her into. White, the colour of innocence, the symbol of inexperience.

Nerves arrived, cold and urgent, to gnaw at the edges of her desire.

Sensing her sudden wavering, he closed his hands over her shoulders, his possessive touch warming her inside and out. 'You're breathtaking. I want you, *amante*, more than I've wanted anyone in a long time.'

She shivered at the intensity, the harsh purpose in his voice. She didn't doubt the veracity of his statement. Only her ability to reciprocate even an ounce of that purpose. And then there was that vein of disillusionment in his eyes. She knew it needed addressing.

'Alejandro, can we…clear the air?' she ventured.

Coldness momentarily washed over his features. 'No, *amante*. You're about to be mine. By the time I'm done with you, you'll forget every single thing about him. But until that happens, there will be no discussion, *entiendes*?' he bit out roughly.

She shook her head. 'Please—'

His thumb on her lower lip stilled her words. He took her hand, placed it on his chest, over his strong, *racing* heartbeat. 'Feel what you do to me, even before we're in bed together. You kiss me like you need me, like you're on fire for me—'

'I do,' she asserted, her voice clear and certain. 'I am.'

A deep shudder ran through him, transmitting through his thundering heartbeat. Dropping his head, he brushed his lips against hers. 'That, Elise, is all I need.'

She allowed relief to wash away the doubt, aware that she was also buying her heart a little time before it was totally devastated. Because once she explained her reasons for Kyoto, she would be laid bare.

Standing on her tiptoes, she deepened the kiss, which he allowed her for a few dizzying heartbeats. Then his primal dominance took over.

Turning her in his arms, he traced his hands down her side and over her waist to cradle her hips. When a soft, hot kiss landed at the base of her spine, she shivered, even while her skin tightened and tingled with the most delicious pleasure.

Sure fingers hooked into her panties and drew them down her legs, his fingers lingering in places she hadn't known were sensitive. Her shoes followed, and then she was naked. Naked and exposed to the man who held her heart in his hands without knowing it.

She sensed him rise behind her, felt the towering wall of his lust engulf her.

'Turn around, *mi corazón*,' he growled, his voice

barely recognisable, but at the same time empowering her.

Slowly, she turned, met his bold, burning gaze. Something shifted in his eyes. She wanted to hope that it was an emotion akin to that which moved through her, but then his gaze swept down, possessing her, branding her.

'*Tu es magnífico,*' he grated roughly.

'And you…you have too many clothes on,' she whispered brokenly.

His rough laugh broke the spellbinding moment. But only for a second. In the next breath, the air thickened again, unspoken wishes and frenzied desire whipping around them even though he took his time to shrug off his jacket and step out of his shoes.

It was like her own personal striptease show; she watched, totally captivated as he undid the buttons of his shirt. Golden skin, a chiselled torso dusted with silky hair became her prize. Heat flooded her entire being, before centring hard and hot between her thighs. By the time he lowered his zip and tugged down his trousers and boxer briefs, Elise was certain she'd lost the ability to breathe. He was big and proud and utterly beautiful.

'Alejandro…'

He closed his eyes for a second, as if gathering

in his control. When he opened them again and speared her with green fire, he was once again in command. He caught her hand and led her to the king-size bed, stretched her out on it, then reached into his bedside drawer. At the sight of the condoms, she blushed.

He laughed almost cruelly as he stretched out beside her, his fingers tracing her heated cheeks. 'Am I insane to still love your blushes?'

'Yes. I hate them.'

'As much as I'd love another battle of words with you, right now, *amante*, I crave your kiss even more. Kiss me, Elise.'

With a moan torn from the very soul of her, she wrapped her arms around his neck and satisfied their need. Within seconds the drugging kiss had set her on a course from which she didn't want to return. Alejandro's hands explored, gripping, demanding, lingering, and moulding until her moans threaded together in a continuous litany.

Then his fingers breached the heart of her. Her eyes flew open, her breath catching as pleasure arrowed, swift and lethal, between her thighs. Teasing the bundle of nerves, he dipped lower, one finger sliding inside.

He groaned, and swallowed hard. '*Dios, so wet. So tight.*'

She shuddered as he pulled out and slid back in. 'Oh!' A different set of emotions gathered, a promise of something transcendental on the horizon that shimmered just beyond her reach. Heart hammering, she strained for it, groaning in protest when Alejandro's finger left her.

His trailing mouth on her skin made up for it though, until she sensed his destination.

Her head jerked off the pillow. 'Alejandro, no...'

Molten eyes speared hers as his shoulders parted her thighs. 'Yes. Save your breath, *querida*. I intend to win this argument, too.'

He didn't ease her into pleasure. Alejandro dropped her hard and screaming into it. Emotion she came to recognise as bliss engulfed her seconds later as she climaxed, wild and free and shattered, against his open-mouthed kisses.

She floated down, vaguely aware of his hot, sweat-sheened skin beneath her hands. But slowly, her senses sparked once more, her body responding to the demands of his hands and the pressure of the body braced above hers.

He parted her thighs, positioned himself at her core. His eyes locked on her face. And she glimpsed the look again.

He started to lean down. She placed a hand on his chest.

'Wait.'

He froze, his breathing harsh, teeth clenched. 'Elise, *por favor*, now is not the time—'

'Yes, it *is*. I didn't... Nothing happened with... In Kyoto,' she stammered.

Shock built in his eyes, but there was also scepticism. 'You don't need to say that to appease me,' he bit out.

She shook her head. 'But it's the truth, Alejandro. I'm still a virgin.'

He stared deep into her eyes, his gaze piercingly raw. Whatever he saw in her face made his chest heave. 'Elise...' His voice rumbled away like distant thunder.

He didn't need her reassurance. She knew he saw the truth in her face. But she gave it anyway. Reaching up, she placed her hand on his cheek. 'I'm still untouched, Alejandro. Make me yours?'

The arms braced on either side of her trembled as the last trace of harshness trailed away from his face to leave fierce, ravenous hunger.

His kiss was deep and rough and intense, as if he meant to consume her completely.

When he lifted his head, her excitement was cresting a fever pitch.

She swallowed as his gaze latched on hers. '*Lo siento, querida*. I'm sorry. This cannot be helped.'

Biting her lips, she nodded.

'Hold on to me,' he rasped.

She complied, her hands finding purchase on his muscled shoulders and holding tight. Before she could take another breath he penetrated her, sliding in deep and sure.

Pain jerked through her, sharp and primal, ripping a scream from her.

Above her, Alejandro hissed and held himself still. '*Dios*, are you all right?'

She blinked through prickling tears and struggled to speak. 'Y...yes.'

He kissed her again, a gentle anointing and a promise of things to come. The pain receded, leaving behind the reality of the power and fullness of him inside her. He moved. Her nails dug deeper into his skin as a different sensation thrummed inside. His hips rolled again. Intoxicating pleasure lanced through her, dragging her eyelids down.

'No. Look at me,' he instructed. 'Feel me. *Feel what you do to me.*'

Her gaze reconnected with his. Exhaling, he increased the tempo, and she cried out. 'Oh...*yes!*'

The word seemed to breach a dam inside him. With a guttural groan, he sealed his mouth to hers, his tongue commencing a brazen mimicry of what his body was doing to hers. Elise could only attempt to keep up as he set her on a trajectory of pleasure so overwhelming her cries grew into a scream, right before sheer bliss catapulted her into a different dimension.

Alejandro watched her, unable to take his eyes off her radiant beauty as her pleasure overtook her. She was already proving to be a responsive lover; her eyes didn't once stray from his, a deed he found almost too much to bear when his pleasure surged high. Higher than he'd ever felt before. For one wild second he wondered if it was because she'd confessed her innocence at a crucial stage. He didn't deny the declaration had filled him with a primal emotion that had left him raw and exposed. That beast still prowled through him, urging him to possess, to stake his claim here and now.

But no. This feeling of heightened awareness and existing on a visceral realm had existed between them long before they'd stepped into his bedroom.

The sex had just brought it to the fore.

But now it was here? Now he'd had a taste of it? *Dios*, he wanted to die in it. Alejandro spiked his fingers into her hair, angled her head to receive his deeper kiss, the feeling of falling, losing himself in her tight heat a drug he never wanted to be freed from.

Her legs clamped tighter around his waist, urging him on, welcoming him home. A harsh groan ripped from his throat. And he allowed himself to fall.

CHAPTER THIRTEEN

ELISE WOKE UP some hours later to the feel of a warm towel drifting over her skin. Blinking awake, she blushed at the sight of Alejandro perched naked on the side of the bed, tending to her.

'You don't need to do that,' she blurted.

A slow, sexy smile lit his face, drawing her absorbed attention to the delicious stubble gracing his jaw. 'No, I don't. But doing it pleases me.'

He grasped her knee and spread her wider. Elise's hands flew up to cover her face, shaking her head wildly as a full body blush engulfed her.

Alejandro laughed. After a minute, he said, 'Open your eyes, *guapa*. The ordeal is over.'

She dragged her hand down her face to see him toss the washcloth away. 'That can't happen again. Ever.'

His smile was arrogantly confident and blatantly possessive. 'I have extensive and uninhibited plans for your body, *amante*. After-sex care should be the least of your worries.'

Prowling over her, he took her mouth in a long,

mind-melting kiss. 'Do I have a say in these plans at all?'

His mouth drifted down her collarbone, planting kisses on her skin. 'Only when it comes to vocalising your pleasure.'

She cringed. 'I seriously doubt that will happen.'

He smiled against her skin. 'Is that a challenge?'

A sliver of ice cooled her desire. 'No. It's not.'

Alejandro's head jerked up. 'What's wrong?'

Elise shook her head. 'It's nothing…I don't want to ruin the…this.'

'Then tell me what's wrong.'

'What you said about being vocal…it was another of those *motherly* pieces of advice I received when…' She pressed her lips together. 'Can we change the subject, please?'

'No.' Alejandro rose and planted his hands on either side of her head. 'It's time to end this.'

'Alejandro—'

'You have severe hang-ups about your sexuality. Which is understandable considering the less-than-stellar guidance you were given regarding your body. Your parents tried to turn what should be a natural expression of desire into a commodity to be peddled. You denied them the power to do that by choosing how you used your body. You're beautiful, *querida*.' He punctuated the compliment with a kiss. 'You have nothing to be ashamed or embarrassed about. When we made love, you held nothing back. You fell apart in my arms and that's how I want you, every time. Telling your lover what you want in bed doesn't demean you, especially if he wants it, too. *Sí?*'

Elise didn't realise tears had welled up until she blinked. When they rolled down her eyes, he brushed them away. 'Yes.'

'Good.'

He kissed her, soft and sweet. Then he rolled them over so she was poised above him. 'Now, to demonstrate, here comes your first instruction. Brace your hands on the headboard.'

She glanced up at the smooth, silk-lined board that extended halfway up the wall. 'I… What?'

His grin was pure wickedness. 'I didn't stutter.'

When she continued to stare in puzzlement and trepidation, he gripped her waist and pulled her up until her torso was suspended above him, her breasts a tantalising inch from his mouth.

With a deep groan, he parted his lips and closed them over one nipple. Elise gasped, her hands seeking the solid reassurance of the headboard as white-hot pleasure seared her.

After an age he freed her bud, and licked her

areola. 'I've wanted to do this since the day you walked into my office.'

'Just this?' she asked, her voice a breathless mess.

A sexy smile formed around her aching nipple. 'Oh, no, *amante*. But this was what I had in mind for starters. Hours and *hours* of this.' His tongue flicked rapidly over her heated flesh, sending spears of need straight to her core. Fingers digging into the headboard, she gave in to the insane urge to look down, see what he was doing. The visual sensation was even more intense as he switched his attention to her neglected nipple.

'That sounds...dangerously mind-altering,' she whispered.

Merciless teeth nipped. 'You've had me in a state for a while. It's only fair that I reciprocate.' He nipped again.

'Alejandro!'

He groaned. '*Sí*, say my name like that.'

She repeated his name because she couldn't form any other words. And because beneath her, his flesh thickened against her thigh each time she said his name. Power, feminine and wicked, surged through her. For a moment, she was ashamed of it, certain it was similar to that which her mother had honed and wielded for as long as Elise could remember.

'I hope you're not trying to induce a different form of mind-alteration by thinking about anything else but what's happening in this bed right now?' Alejandro growled.

Elise shook herself free of the intrusive thoughts. 'No. I wouldn't dare.'

Alejandro lifted an eyebrow. 'You and I both know you would. You've been daring me since the day we met.'

'Okay, maybe I would, but I want you more than I want to risk you stopping what you're doing. So I surrender.'

His eyes flared for a single, gripping moment. Reaching across, he plucked a condom from the table. His gaze still trapping hers, he slid it on, positioned her in place and gripped her waist.

'Time for your next lesson. And, Elise?'

'Yes?' she gasped, her senses already on fire as his powerful erection probed her core.

He entered her in one smooth thrust, his teeth clenched on a guttural groan. Only when he was fully seated inside her did he continue.

'You will not hold back.'

Those five words set the bar for the next few weeks as Alejandro and Gael took the financial world by storm. With a specially selected team, they crisscrossed the globe, setting up satellite offices and factories and vetting other conglomerates who vied to be affiliated with the newly formed Atlas Group that comprised SNV, Toredo and Ishikawa Corporation.

In her role as his PR consultant, Elise was never far from his side during the day. And Alejandro's inexhaustible demands ensured she was even closer to him at night.

The ride was undeniably thrilling, the sex even more so.

But in her rare quiet moments, she couldn't silence the hopeful voice that questioned whether this *could* ever be more than just sex.

Alejandro didn't show signs of tiring of it, which initially helped her to talk herself into believing that what they had was enough.

But with the slow passage of the weeks, and the stark realisation that their working relationship was winding down, fear had taken hold.

There had been no further mention of Kyoto, Alejandro finding effective ways of silencing her whenever she attempted to explain. And she…she'd taken the coward's way out, protecting her heart for a little longer whenever she let him kiss away the subject of why she'd kissed Jason.

His avoidance tactic had bled into the subject

of his family. The few times Gael had mentioned Spain, Alejandro had tensed and changed the subject.

To say he was still aggressively opposed to tackling his past was an understatement.

Which was why she ground to a halt after entering the study of the Kensington mansion they'd rented for their week-long stay in London.

The brothers glared at each other across the large George V desk, the strewn papers indicating tempers had been fraying for a while.

'Umm…should I leave you two alone? I came to inform you that dinner with the Finance Minister is set for tonight, but I can go over the details later if you want?'

Alejandro's gaze locked on her for a studying minute. Rounding the desk, he shut the door and slid his arm around her waist.

His features remained pinched but his flashed smile was genuine. 'No, stay. My brother suffers from selective memory. Perhaps you should hear this, too, so I have a witness down the road the next time he feels like laying into me.'

Gael grimaced, but there was a whisper of apprehension in his expression as he eyed his brother. 'I'm just trying to get a picture of what it was like for you.'

'What good would it do to rehash everything?'

Gael shrugged. 'Maybe none. But if those three weeks I spent looking for my mother were anything like you claim yours were—'

'You think those three weeks were hell? I lived like that from the moment I was born until the day I walked away. Count yourself lucky you only got to spend a limited amount of time with our father, Gael. When he wasn't playing away, he taunted my mother with the possibility of it. When he did stray, she tortured herself and everyone around her with her desperate unhappiness.'

Elise's breath punched out in desperate sympathy.

Shock glinted in Gael's eyes. *'Madre de Dios.'*

Alejandro walked her over to the grouping of sofas set before a roaring fire in the oak-panelled room and pulled Elise down next to him. Gael joined them, settling on the opposite sofa.

November in London was picturesque and quint-essentially autumnal, with a light drizzle hitting the giant Victorian windows. But as much as she wanted to stand at the window and absorb every-thing British, staying at Alejandro's side as he al-lowed his rigid facade to crack for a moment was the only place she wanted to be.

'If ever there were two people more unsuited to each other, it was them. I used to go to bed at night praying they would tell me in the morning that they were divorcing.' A rough laugh barked from his throat. The sound tore at Elise. Leaning closer, she placed a hand on his chest. After a moment, he absently covered hers with his.

'While children around the world wished upon stars that their parents would stay together through thick and thin, I yearned for the opposite. Both sets of my grandparents were dead, my remaining relatives were spread far and wide, but I didn't give a damn where I ended up. All I wanted was for the hell I lived in to be over.'

'Alejandro, you can't hate yourself for wishing for a better life. None of us can.'

He blinked, several emotions drifting through his eyes. 'What about hating one's own parents? Is that allowed?'

'*Sí*, it's allowed,' Gael uttered grimly.

Elise sensed he was going through his own issues regarding his parentage, but her only focus right then was Alejandro

'The only person who can truly judge you is you. You're also the only one who can determine how the past influences you. You told me that, remember?'

He shook his head, his smile tinged with sadness. 'It's not the same, *amante*.'

She lifted her eyebrow. 'Isn't it?'

His eyes darkened. 'I won't be drawn into a debate, Elise. Not on this.' The warning was clear. His mind was made up about the subject. But he caught his brother's gaze from across the table. 'I admit, I made you into a villain, too, in that hellish reality, Gael. Back then, I believed you and your mother contributed to the problem.' He shook his head. 'But only one person is to blame for this. And it's not you.' His voice was solemn, his gaze as beseeching as an inherently proud and autocratic man could achieve.

Emotion rippled across Gael's face. He swallowed hard. Nodded silent acceptance. Then he surged to his feet and gathered up a sheaf of documents. 'I'll go through these before our meeting with the minister,' he said gruffly, then left the room.

'My father had wanted a son, someone he could pass on his well-honed cut-throat business skills to. Did I tell you that?' She spoke into the silence several minutes later.

Alejandro's chest rose and fell in a mildly frustrated manner. 'Elise...'

'My mother told me when I was twelve or thirteen and was refusing to wear some dress she'd bought me. I was a mistake my father convinced her to keep so he could pass on the family legacy. She'd

refused to have any more children who would interrupt her career in prestige acquisition. They wanted
a son and they got me instead. A daughter with
ideals so far removed from theirs, I once heard them
wonder out loud whether I was really their child.'

'*Dios,*' he swore under his breath.

'You're not the only one who wished for different
parents. But what you feel in here—' she tapped
his chest and the strong heart beating beneath it
'—won't go away if you don't confront it.'

Green eyes pierced hers, probing. Suddenly afraid
he would see too much, she dropped her gaze.

'Come here, Elise.'

Since she was already sitting pretty darn close,
she wondered what he meant. He resolved her con-
fusion by picking her up and settling her in his lap.
His fingers removed the clasp in her hair and let
the heavy tresses cascade around her face.

After pulling her into a long kiss, he set her back.
'*Gracias,*' he murmured.

'What for?'

His expression grew brooding, introspective.
'I will know soon enough. But thank you,' he repeated.

Her heart lurched at the depth of emotion behind
the words. And even though she told herself it was

futile to read anything into it, she found herself
smiling.

'Okay.'

Emotion of a different, specific nature entered
his eyes. His hand tightened at her waist as he devoured her smile. 'Feel like relocating upstairs for
an hour or two before this meeting?' he rasped.

Her nod brought him to his feet. He didn't release
her, instead walked out of the study and up to their
bedroom with her locked in his arms.

And as he made love to her with a fevered, almost spiritual need, Elise wondered why she'd ever
thought she could feel anything other than soul-
searing love for this man.

Alejandro stilled in the act of securing his cufflink.

'Repeat that, if you please.'

Elise groaned and rolled her eyes, but it gratified
him to see apprehension in her eyes. She was wise
to be apprehensive. Because the words she'd just
spoken threatened to rip a gaping hole somewhere
in the region of his heart. He knew it couldn't be
the actual organ that was affected, because that
wasn't what they were dealing with here. Hearts
and flowers and gentle words weren't part of their
deal. Despite the decision he'd come to in the week

since the study incident, those softer things would never feature in his life.

Nevertheless, a hole threatened. A deep black hole where emotions like desolation, despair, *pain* resided.

'Don't be upset, Alejandro. I made a promise. I have to keep it.'

He felt the ground beneath him shift. It was infinitesimal, but it registered. 'A promise?'

She sighed. 'Yes, you know those occasions where you pledge something and then you have to honour it?'

'I know the definition,' he murmured. 'I was very much aware of the existence of promises as a child but sadly I never got to experience anyone either making or keeping one.'

She paused in the act of tying the strings of a wraparound dress around her waist.

'I'm sorry, Alejandro.' Soft compassion blazed from her eyes and warmed him. Everything inside him strained to be closer to that sensation. To lose himself in it and let it wash away the cold loneliness that had been a part of him for so long he didn't remember a time when it hadn't existed.

'*De nada,*' he responded, aware his voice was gruff. Flicking his cuffs, he attempted to thread the links through again. Realising his hands shook, he slammed the studs on the dressing table. 'I'm still waiting for an explanation.'

'It's my grandmother's birthday this weekend. I always spend it with her. She expects me to be there.'

Alejandro noticed he was rubbing a precise spot on his chest where his heart thudded dully and transferred his fingers to the equally insistent throb at his temple. He had to tread carefully. He knew that. The last thing he wanted was to be drawn into an argument with Elise. But… 'She's in Hawaii, correct?'

She nodded warily.

'And I…' He searched for words that wouldn't make him feel so raw…so *exposed*. In the end the words poured out regardless. 'I need you here,' he rasped.

She crossed the dressing room and stopped in front of him. Her hand slid up his chest to curl around his nape. 'I'm sorry I can't come with you to Seville. But you were always going to make this final journey on your own anyway.'

His jaw clenched. '*Sí*, but not while you were on the other side of the world!'

'Alejandro—'

He whirled away from her, unable to stand having her in front of him and knowing it was only for a short time. Striding through the bedroom, he stepped out onto the warm terrace.

On the horizon, the sun was setting over the hills just outside Barcelona. During one of their recent and increasingly frequent talks, Gael had spoken of his estate outside Barcelona and the neighbouring property that had just come on the market.

Alejandro had bought the fifty-thousand-acre estate, sight unseen. When Gael had thrown in the offer of his architect and interior designer, Alejandro had agreed.

His first visit to his property three days ago had been a pleasant surprise, especially when Elise had seemed to love the estate, too.

The whitewashed villa was vast, with staggered floors on three levels, each with a wraparound terrace that overlooked a private beach. It was a house that had a potential to be a home.

From a personal standpoint, it had been a place to pause and regroup before taking the final step back in time.

Because as Elise had counselled, he had to revisit the past in order to move on. Some aspects of his childhood had left scars he was certain would never heal, but he needed to find out if other building blocks he'd thought were eroded were in fact merely shrouded with bitterness.

Things like love and trust...

Alejandro knew he most likely wouldn't find those two components in his childhood home, but perhaps freeing himself from other entanglements would open his eyes to new experiences.

New emotions?

But how could he see his way to finding answers when Elise was leaving? *Dios.* He rubbed at his chest when he sensed her behind him.

'We're going to be late to the dinner with the vintner.'

'We're not going.'

She sighed. 'Why not?'

He turned and leaned against the terrace wall, his back to the view. Right now the only view he was interested in was the one before him. 'Because he's another fat cat hoping to get fatter by riding on Atlas's coattails. He can wait one more day. Whereas you...' He stalked to where she stood, her stunning face glowing in the evening light.

'Yes...me?' she invited huskily.

He wrapped his hands loosely around her throat, sliding his thumbs under her chin to tilt her face up to his. 'You are making me *extremely* unhappy with your impending departure,' he said.

Her breath hitched and her arms slid around his waist. 'And you mean to punish me?' she asked.

Alejandro was marginally satisfied with the raw anticipation on her face. She wanted him with almost as much intensity as he craved her. It wasn't anywhere near enough, but that would have to sustain him in her absence.

'Yes, I do.' He pulled on the ties to her dress none too gently, and tugged the material from her body, leaving her clad in scraps of black lace. Alejandro wasn't worried about exposing her to unwelcome eyes. The position of the terrace guaranteed them complete privacy. As he stepped back his knees nearly buckled at her beauty. 'Your punishment will be very specific, *guapa*. And very, very thorough.'

He dispensed with foreplay, his need soul-wrenchingly acute. He left her only to locate a condom. When he returned, he placed her on her knees, dispensed of his clothes, and took her hard and fast. Groans turned to earthy demands, moans to cries of ecstasy. Somewhere in the middle of it all, Alejandro acknowledged that he would never get enough of her.

Hours later, he tucked her close, his fingers teasing through her hair as sweat cooled on their bodies.

She had given back as good as he dished out, but he knew the depth of his lovemaking tonight had

worn her out. Her soft breathing told him she was
almost asleep. A part of him wanted to keep the
status quo. But a greater part of him felt the need
to relax the reins of his control for her, even if it
made him vulnerable.

'I'd never experienced jealousy before I met you.
Now I'm jealous of every single moment you'll
spend away from me.'

A soft gasp broke from her. 'Alejandro.'

'How long?' he grated. He kept his gaze fixed on
the ceiling, absurdly unwilling to risk looking into
her eyes in that moment.

'Three days. Four at the most.'

He swallowed hard. 'Take my plane.'

'What? No, you need it—'

'Gael arrives tomorrow. He'll no doubt resume
his efforts to remain a pain in my backside. He can
fly me down to Seville on Saturday.'

'I—'

He captured a handful of silky hair. 'Say "thank
you, Alejandro."'

'Thank you, *Oh, Bossy One.*'

He kissed her, because the time had long since
passed when he could resist her. As passion whipped
high and fierce again, Alejandro wondered if it was
past time to stop trying to save his heart from big-
ger, riskier things, as well.

* * *

He ended up catching a commercial flight to Seville when Gael got caught up in an emergency. The mundane nature of it all helped keep his mind off the impending visit. And off the sheer intensity with which he missed Elise.

There were more satellite factories to set up and contracts to negotiate with new businesses, but from the start there'd been an unspoken agreement between them that this affair would only last for the duration of her contract with him.

Which meant that she would be gone in a few weeks. Or it had been that way. Until he'd woken this morning with a physical pain in his chest from missing her.

Alejandro didn't have anything to compare these emotions to, but whatever he felt for her, he knew he wasn't ready to walk away. And their goodbye in his plane two days ago had given him hope that she felt the same way.

All he had to do was lay a few ghosts to rest—

'Andro.'

He stopped in his tracks. The voice. The name. *Dios*, it dragged him back to a place he suddenly doubted he wanted to go.

Slowly he turned to his left. And exhaled at the sight of his father.

A tumult of emotions tore through him, cracking open places he'd thought were sealed for ever. *'Papá.'*

Tomas Aguilar held out his hand. Alejandro hesitated for a moment, then stepped forward and took it.

'We need to talk.'

The older man, who despite his greying hair and slightly stooped posture still turned female heads, nodded. '*Sí,* I don't imagine you came all this way just to sample the sangria.' He looked down at Alejandro's empty hand. 'No bags?'

'I'm not staying.'

Regret and sadness passed through his father's eyes. Although he steeled himself against it, Alejandro was buoyed by that show of emotion.

The sudden need to find *some* redeemable quality within himself didn't pass without ironic notice. He followed his father into the cool sunshine.

The ride to his childhood home was conducted mostly in silence. When his father drew up in front of the villa, Alejandro couldn't bring himself to step out.

The two-storey structure had been modernised over the years, a fresh coat of paint added recently. But it was still the same home where he'd witnessed and known despair and desolation. Where he'd lived in fear of flying missiles and broken trust.

'You won't find the answers you need sitting in the car, Andro. You may not even find answers inside, but at least make the attempt.'

His father got out and rounded the bonnet. Sucking in a breath, Alejandro followed suit. As they neared the front door it opened. A half-sob, half-gasp sounded from within a second before his mother appeared.

Evita Aguilar had aged with grace. And despite the similar sadness that lurked in her eyes, she carried herself with a quiet pride.

'Andro, *mi chico*,' she murmured. She held out her arms.

He stepped into the embrace, and felt another crack in his chest. He allowed himself to be drawn inside, bustled over and fed.

But eventually, his restlessness resurfaced. His father grabbed a bottle of wine, his mother brought glasses and they settled on the small terrace that abutted the garden.

As it happened, Alejandro didn't need to ask the questions burning in his heart.

'We made your life hell,' his father said gravely.

'Yes,' he responded.

Tomas glanced at his wife and the look they

shared jarred something harder within Alejandro. 'We had access to marriage counsellors, and divorce courts. Perhaps you want to know why we never made use of them.'

Alejandro swallowed hard, the shame at admitting his secret wish profound. 'Yes.'

'That answer is simple. We stayed together because we love each other. Despite the tumult. Despite it not making sense to others, even sometimes to us.' Tomas reached for his wife's hand. 'No one has the right to judge us, or tell us how to love. Time and wisdom have helped us see the light in some ways, but in other ways we wouldn't change a thing. So if you came here seeking rationality, or a straightforward, risk-free way to love your woman—and I know all this is because of a woman; you're my son after all—we have no answers for you. You'll have to find your own way.'

Shock scythed through Alejandro, followed closely by an absurd understanding. He didn't know if what he felt for Elise was love, but it was certainly beyond his comprehension. And he'd been prepared to risk a business deal in order to hang on to it.

He didn't know what his next steps would be, but he was willing to take the leap. A knot in his gut eased and his next breath came easier.

'There are some things that we never forgave ourselves for, though,' his mother said, her hazel eyes pleading with his. 'We should've made sure you knew you were loved. I should've protected you more from my...insecurities. Losing you the way we did...' A sob caught in her throat and his father passed her a tissue.

'We probably have no right to ask you for forgiveness. But we would like you to consider it,' his father said.

Alejandro swallowed again to displace the rock in his throat. Rising, he bent down and kissed his mother's cheek. 'I'll consider it, *Mamá*. Goodbye.'

She caught and held on to his hand. 'Will...will I see you again?'

He'd taken Elise's advice. He'd confronted his past and had found a modicum of understanding.

The apple doesn't fall far from the tree. In some ways that was true.

Some apples fall far enough. In other ways that was also true.

'Yes, you'll see me again.'

CHAPTER FOURTEEN

ALEJANDRO RESISTED THE URGE to catch a flight to Hawaii and returned to Chicago instead.

Twenty-four hours. Elise would be back in his bed before nightfall tomorrow. It was a thought that kept him marginally sane, although Elise sending back his plane because she felt bad about it 'just sitting there doing nothing' irritated him in the extreme.

He looked up from the document he'd read for the last half-hour without taking a single word in, and accepted the espresso Sergio set before him.

'Do we know the weather forecast for Hawaii at this time of year? You haven't heard of any cyclones or tornados reported in that part of the world, have you?'

'No, *señor*. As far as I know the weather is copacetic over there.'

Alejandro tossed back the espresso. 'Good. She's been gone a week. I don't want anything interrupting her flight back.'

'Uh, she's been gone three days, *señor*.'

Alejandro glared at him and rose from the dining table. 'Don't you have something to be getting on with?'

He ignored his butler's sly smirk as he headed out to his car.

Three hours later he was reading the same document in his office, without success. He'd instituted a 'No calls bar Elise's' policy with Margo, but with each minute his phone remained silent, his irritation grew.

He abandoned reading when Margo knocked and offered to get his lunch. His *no* was a touch less than polite.

'Apologies, Margo. Thanks, but I'm not hungry,' he tried again. She nodded and turned to leave.

'Are you sure my phone is working?' he demanded.

She frowned. 'Um…yes, I think so.'

'You *think* so? Get the IT guys down here to take a look, would you?'

She cleared her throat. 'There's nothing wrong with your phone, sir. I'm *sure* of it.'

Alejandro picked up his cell phone and checked it. Full signal. He tossed it back.

'She's been gone for a week. Would it kill her to call at least *once* today?' he muttered.

'Sir…she's been gone three days.'

A tic throbbed at his temple. 'Why does everyone feel the need to keep correcting me?' he snapped.

Margo hid a grin and hurried out.

Alejandro's mood had in no way improved when he left his office to attend a meeting mid-afternoon. His half a dozen calls to Elise had gone straight to voicemail. And he'd realised that at no point had he thought it prudent to take her grandmother's number.

What use were all the introspection and realisations he'd come to if he couldn't share them with her immediately? And why wasn't she missing him enough to call him umpteen times the way his exes used to? A sludge of shame welled at the unkind thought.

He loved Elise because she was like no other.

Alejandro stilled on his way out of the business tower where his meeting had taken place and let the words sink in.

He loved her...

With every pump of his heart, the truth blazed brighter. Sheer, unadulterated emotion charged through him. For the first time in his life, he let it in and felt a rush so strong, so deep, he feared his heart would expire from the fullness.

He couldn't lie—it scared him. But on the flip side, it had the potential to fulfil him as nothing ever had in his life.

He just needed Elise back. Now. Reaching into

his pocket, he pulled out his phone. He dialled, held the phone to his ear.

Someone bumped into him. 'Sorry, excuse me.'

Alejandro smiled, his newfound outlook on life allowing him to be accommodating. 'Elise, *Madre de Dios*, pick up—'

The words died in his throat as he stared across the vast, busy foyer to the trendy restaurant housed within the building.

It was Elise. Even on the extremely unlikely chance that his eyesight deceived him, her smile and accompanying laugh a second later reached inside him and touched the heart he'd discovered moments ago belonged to her.

Alejandro dragged his gaze from her face to stare down at his phone. It was ringing. It hadn't gone to voicemail like before. He looked back up in time to see her make the *one second* signal at her lunch companion. She reached into her bag, took out her phone. Saw his number, and dropped it back.

Ice drenched him from head to toe. In all his life, Alejandro had never felt the fear or desolation that struck his heart in that moment. He'd dared to take the risk, even before he knew he loved her. The knowledge of exactly what he felt for her made the heartache a million times worse. He stood there. He stared.

And he knew why his world had turned to ash.

She talked. She flipped her hair. Her smile was radiance itself.

Bile rose in his gut, threatened to choke him. Almost on automatic, he called again.

It went straight to voicemail.

Alejandro turned and walked out into the sunshine on numb legs.

He was sitting in the dark sitting room *two hours* later when he heard the click of the electronic lock. He'd given Sergio the night off to save the butler from the fallout of his impending devastation.

She sailed in and dropped her small suitcase on the floor.

'Honey, I'm home!' She giggled. She *giggled.* 'I've always wanted to say that ridiculous line.'

Her handbag followed and she hurried across the room to where he sat, an empty whisky glass clutched in his hand.

'Oh, Alejandro, I missed you so much!' She launched herself into his arms, knocking the glass to the floor. Her arms slid around his neck and her head slanted towards his. His breath snagged painfully, his insides going from ice-cold to furnace-hot just from the scent of her. 'Enough to change my flight to an earlier one. Enough to ignore why you're sitting here, drinking in the dark. I don't care why. I need to kiss you. Right now.'

Her mouth latched onto his. And in the second

between killing himself to pull away and completing the act, he noted her confidence, her skill at kissing. The enticing way she moved her body over him. Just the way he'd taught her.

He wanted to latch on hard. He wanted to bind himself to her so she could never be free of him.

But he couldn't.

He ripped his head away from her, his arms holding her back.

'We need to talk, Elise.'

Her mouth went slack, her eyes widening into pools of shock before she composed herself and nodded. Climbing from his lap, she took a seat across from him. 'No good thing ever came from those words, but okay. Shoot.'

Alejandro had had enough time to run through several thousand scenarios of how this would go. For a thousand different reasons he'd discarded all of them.

'This isn't working for me.' False words. *Freeing* words.

Her breath audibly caught, and her hand rose to rest over her heart before she swallowed hard. 'Right. I… Okay. I…wish you'd emailed or texted me or something. I wouldn't have bothered you here…' Her chin dropped down, her hair momentarily shielding her face as she toyed with her fingers.

'Breaking up by text is uncouth.'

A sharp laugh barked from her. '*Uncouth?* Okay. Well, I wouldn't know. This is my first break-up.' She winced.

Alejandro grimaced, then got ahold of himself. He was doing this for *her*.

Then why did he feel as if he'd cut out his own heart?

Because he had.

She jumped up. 'Well, I guess that's it, then.'

He surged to his feet. '*That's it?*' His world was to end without so much as a thunderclap?

Eyes filled with hurt and the beginnings of anger finally met his. 'Why, what do you expect? Funeral bagpipes? Sorry, you'll have to be disappointed—'

'I saw you today,' he flung at her. 'At the Wood-bine Building.'

She frowned for a second, then her face cleared. 'And?'

'*And?* You expect an addendum to that?'

Her eyes misted, but she blinked quickly. 'Only if you think I'm owed one. This is your show after all. But maybe you'll allow me three guesses? I saw you at the Woodbine Building having lunch, *and* you have spinach in your teeth so maybe you should go brush? Or, *and* I love the dress you're wearing but I've missed you like crazy and I'm dying to make love to you so I'm going to rip it off right now? Or is it more like, *and* I don't trust you, not even for one hot little second, so *sayonara* and have a nice life?'

Alejandro opened his mouth to give voice to the terrible pain tearing at his insides, but it was as if his vocal cords were suddenly paralysed.

'No answer? Fine, have it your way.' She stormed out of the living room towards the bedroom they'd shared for the last six weeks.

Alejandro charged after her. Only to stop when he found her frozen in the doorway. She whirled around when she sensed him. 'I...I can't go in there. I know this is absurd, but this is my first break-up. I'm not handling it well. If it isn't too much trouble, have my things put into storage...somewhere. I'll text you a forwarding address once I have one.'

She headed for him, making sure to keep a distance between them.

The words tore from his throat. 'I trust you.'

She froze. 'What?'

'You think this is about my lack of trust. But that's just it. I trust you with my life. But I don't know if you can trust me with yours.'

'What on earth are you talking about?'

'I barely noticed who you were having lunch with. But I saw you look at your phone. And ignore my call. It may be irrational to you, but the thought that I might never be enough for you... You know why I never asked you about Jason?'

Numbly, she shook her head.

'I was terrified you'd say you'd compared us and decided he was a better bet,' he divulged. 'I don't want to know what happened with him after I left. All I know is that I had to come and find you. I dragged you back to Chicago with the knowledge that for whatever reason, you chose him. And then I found out you were back, in Montana, and that you *stayed away* after coming back.'

'Alejandro—!'

'I can't do that to you any more. I'm obsessed with you, Elise. I know what that kind of obsession can do. I saw it with my parents. Their love may not make much sense to me, but it's the version they're happy with. I've been sitting in the dark, trying to imagine what our version would be. And in each one, I can't help but see me hurting you. With my jealousy. With my possessiveness. Hell, I want you all the time! I tried to find answers from my parents. The best I got was that love doesn't make sense. That's not good enough. I can't risk you like that. So I thought I'd spare us both the messiness that would come later.'

She absorbed his words, then nodded. 'Okay. I get it. It makes sense.' She started to walk away again.

Naked fear gripped him. 'Elise!'

'Yes, Alejandro?'

'I… *Por favor*…say something.'

'Sorry, I have nothing. You make a sound case. I can't compete with all the bad things that might happen to us in the future.'

He frowned. 'But…you came back from Hawaii early.'

'Yes.'

'Because you missed me?'

'Like crazy.'

He slashed a frustrated hand through his hair. 'Then why didn't you call?'

'I turned my phone to flight mode, then forgot to turn it back on until I was on the subway. Before I could call you, I got a message from one of the five manga publishers I'd sent my sketches to. They'd been trying to reach me. I called them back. They were interested and wanted to meet me right away. I agreed to a meet. He wanted to go through each story with me. I was in the middle of begging him to reschedule our meeting for another time when you called. I ignored your call because I was already being rude and I couldn't tell whether he would accommodate me or not. After an hour and a half, I came clean and told him I missed the man I love and wanted to get back to him. This guy got engaged two weeks ago, so he's all about true love. Of course, I hightailed it here only for you to break up with me. You want to know the real reason I kissed Jason?'

His heart stuttered, the vice around his chest so painful with the glaring loss he'd brought on himself that he couldn't breathe. 'No, but go on.'

'I kissed him because it was the only way I could think of to stop myself from falling deeper in love with you. You said your heart wasn't made to love. I believed you. But I knew it wouldn't stop me from loving you. I was trying to think of how to stop my heart from breaking when Jason found me. The kiss was stupid. I hated every second of it. But seeing you walk away…that was the worst moment of my life. Until Montana. I didn't have to come back with you. I could've let you sue me. But I loved you. I still love you. So tell me, Alejandro, what am I supposed to do with all this love I have bursting in my heart for you, when you're so ready to throw us away?' she whispered, her voice a ragged caricature of its normal strength.

'Elise… *Dios mio*… Elise. What have I done?' He'd blown it. He knew it in the depths of his soul. He reached for her.

She jerked out of his way, her flared hands holding him at bay. 'No. You want to protect *yourself*. That's fine. Believe it or not, I understand.' This time she didn't turn. She walked backwards, righting herself when she bumped into the console table or a wall.

He followed, because not following would be the same as dying. 'Elise, please listen to me. I wanted to protect *you*. From a love that already feels too much.'

Her backward retreat halted, and the blood drained from her face. 'What?'

'I love you, *dulce mia*. So much. *Too much*. That's the problem!'

Her brow furrowed. 'How can love ever be too much?'

'It can, Elise. I've seen it.' He shook his head, unwilling to risk anything that would make her retreat farther. But how could he not state his deepest fear? 'It can turn ugly. It would kill me if I did that to you.'

She shook her head. 'You won't,' she said, and her voice held a core of steel that made him want to believe her. Almost.

He dragged a hand down his face, trying desperately to calm the panicked pants heaving from him.

'Alejandro.'

He stilled. *'Sí?'*

'The version you're talking about is nothing more than a twisted obsession. If your parents are okay with that, then all you can do is give them your blessing. But the love I want, the one I want to *give* you, is about offering you the best of myself, letting you be the best of *yourself.* Does that include going out of your way to hurt me?'

'No. *Never,*' he breathed.

'Are you willing to give us a chance?'

His heart tripped, the possibilities making him dizzy. 'I want nothing more than to treasure you, *amante.* Every second of every day. I know I handled this all wrong, but if you think we can do this… *Dios*, I'll *do* it. But I admit, I'm terrified. I realised how much I loved you seconds before I saw you. It was no excuse, but from the moment we met I felt as if I stood on a ledge, the sensation of losing my footing a credible threat. But today I realised I'd been looking down, making myself dizzy with distractions when I should've been focusing on what was right in front of me. On you, and on the heights we could achieve together…I'm sorry, *mi amor.* So very sorry.'

Her face crumpled for a fleeting second, and she swallowed. 'God, Alejandro, you ripped my heart out,' she cried.

He lunged for her, dropped to his knees and gripped her hips. 'Forgive me. Please, *Dios mio*, I'm the world's biggest fool. I love you. Please give me another chance?'

Her hand slowly reached out. Touched his brow. His hair. When she traced his cheek, he captured it and kissed her palm. 'I forgive you.'

His groan of relief was hoarse with unshed emotion.

'And, Alejandro?'

'Yes?'

'I love you, too.'

Elise dropped to join him on the floor, her pounding heart now, thankfully, beating from love and bliss, and not the terrifying pain of losing the love of her life. Their kiss held relief, joy, passion, and above all, love. After a lifetime of kissing, he stood and carried her to their bedroom, where he showed her with word and deed how much he loved and cherished her.

As they were drifting into blissful sleep a thought popped into her head.

'Umm, Alejandro?'

'*Sí, mi amor?*' His voice was a lazy, sexy drawl that heated her blood and flooded her with pleasure in all the right places.

'I quit as your PR consultant. As of Thursday morning, I hope to have a new and shiny career.'

'Damn.' His fingers drifted over her skin, his caresses gentle and loving. 'Can I tempt you with another offer?'

She raised her head, stared into mossy green eyes burning with pure, everlasting love. 'That depends. Does it come with perks to die for?'

'No, it comes with perks to *live* for. Perks to love

and cherish, in sickness and in health, until the heavens grant us eternal life amongst the stars.'

Tears stormed her eyes. For the longest time she couldn't breathe. Or speak. 'Alejandro,' she whispered.

His hands framed her face, and he stared deep into her heart. 'Marry me, Elise.'

'Yes. Until eternity.'

* * * * *

Maya Blake's RIVAL BROTHERS
duet continues with
ONE NIGHT WITH GAEL
Available March 2017

If you enjoyed this story, check out
these other great reads from Maya Blake:
THE DI SIONE SECRET BABY
SIGNED OVER TO SANTINO
A DIAMOND DEAL WITH THE GREEK
BRUNETTI'S SECRET SON
Available now!